PENGUIN BOOKS
INFINITE LIVES, INFINITE DEATHS

Douglas James Limpe Candano holds a bachelor's in development studies from the Ateneo de Manila University (Development Studies Departmental Award, Loyola Schools Awards for the Arts in Fiction) and a master's in urban planning from McGill University.

His fiction has won several national level awards, including the Philippines Free Press Literary Award and the Don Carlos Palanca Memorial Award for Literature, and has been published and anthologized in numerous publications and books in the Philippines. He has also written for film and theater, co-writing *Orphea*, which premiered during the 2020 Berlinale, and *Love Is a Dog from Hell*—the closing film of the 2022 Berlin Critics Week, as well as the maximalist musical *Super Macho Anti Kristo! (SMAK!): A Headless 100-Act Opera to Mend All Broken Bicycles of the Universe According to Jarry and Rizal*, which had a run at Berlin's iconic Volksbühne theater in 2022.

Aside from a side career as one of the country's top competitive eaters, he works as a freelance research consultant for development programmes, having worked for initiatives of bilateral and multilateral development institutions, national government agencies, corporate foundations, and civil society organizations. He lives in Metro Manila.

ADVANCE PRAISE FOR
INFINITE LIVES, INFINITE DEATHS

'Douglas Candano's *Infinite Lives, Infinite Deaths* is a riveting assemblage of stories set in an alternative version of Manila where folklore and religion meet history, where the fantastic intertwines with fact. The lens with which the characters herein are depicted makes them appear always larger than life, prone to strange encounters, doomed. In accounts that are at times epistolary and in others mythologizing, Candano has curated for himself a distinct, methodical style and an impeccable sense of world-building. The threaded narratives in this book like to posit themselves as accurate chronicles, in so doing data-mine the real for occasions of inexactness, potential, possibility. This way, Candano pushes against the so-called grain, with brave fiction that further elevates the voice of the Filipino in the new speculative.'

—Joel M. Toledo, author of *Planet Nine: Poems*

'I can't put this shit down. Doug is a fuckin' great storyteller.'
—Norman Wilwayco, author of
Mondomanila and *Migrantik*

'History, commerce, politics, and the supernatural flit in and out of these endlessly inventive stories. Like a modern Scheherazade, Douglas Candano spins tale upon tale in this book of wonders. In one story, he wrote about mead: "It is said that a sip would bring solace to the broke, comfort to the stressed, and laughter to the broken." This book also gives these pleasures to the reader.'

—Danton Remoto, author of *Riverrun: A Novel* and
The Heart of Summer: Stories and Tales

'This is an astonishingly brilliant book. It reveals an author's fecund imagination tethered by seemingly academic discourse that suddenly bursts out at the seams into a hallucinatory world of oxymorons. It is a collection of well-made stories written in a variety of non-fictive modes. The effect is sly, subtle black humor. History is the backdrop, respectfully allowing the fictive action and characters center stage. Language is used in the service of the storytelling. Thus does the author demonstrate his mastery of the short story's conventions. The overall picture is the surreal theater of the absurd that is the Philippines. Ordinary human characters going about their stereotypically Chinoy business transform into phantasmagoric creatures before they inexplicably vanish. Yet we feel they now invisibly hover over our shoulders as we read about their infinite lives and infinite deaths.'

—Rosario Cruz-Lucero, author of
La India, or Island of the Disappeared and *Feast
and Famine: Stories of Negros*

'Douglas Candano's prose blends the precise language of the social scientist and the inspired voice of the storyteller to concoct splendid narratives of curiosities and the fantastic. His stories resound with the true fictions of Jorge Luis Borges and the astonishing fabulae of Italo Calvino and Umberto Eco. They are marked by the erudition of history, philosophy, religion, and science; enlivened by the golden dusts of myth and the magical. The wonder of Candano's narratives lies in his clever control (or a deliberate lack thereof) of time—a reinvention of his own fictional time. Everything occurs in a sphere of simultaneity, in an infinitude of the multiverse. Everything occurs in a transience of places. Such temporal imaginings grant Candano's stories the power of transcendence and timelessness.'

—Shirley Lua, associate professor of
literature and cultural studies at
De La Salle University, Manila, Philippines

Infinite Lives, Infinite Deaths

Douglas Candano

PENGUIN BOOKS

An imprint of Penguin Random House

PENGUIN BOOKS

USA | Canada | UK | Ireland | Australia
New Zealand | India | South Africa | China | Southeast Asia

Penguin Books is part of the Penguin Random House group of companies
whose addresses can be found at global.penguinrandomhouse.com

Published by Penguin Random House SEA Pte Ltd
9, Changi South Street 3, Level 08-01,
Singapore 486361

First published in Penguin Books by Penguin Random House SEA 2024

ISBN 9789815144864

Typeset in Garamond by MAP Systems, Bengaluru, India

www.penguin.sg

Contents

Dreaming Valhalla

While the Church of the Nativity along Katapatan Road is considered a landmark, by no means does it date back to Hispanic times. Despite its arched doorways, stained-glass windows, and stone carvings typical of eighteenth-century Manila, the church was actually constructed in the late 1990s, on the spot where the Valhalla Club used to be until it burned down and its owner, Ericsson Chua, disappeared.

In its heyday, the Valhalla Club was Manila's premier nightclub, where politicians rubbed elbows with lonely expatriates and the sons of Chinese taipans. There, they would drink, dine, and be merry as they stroked the thighs of the lovely Valkyries.

From the outside, the Valhalla Club was nothing special. It was shaped like a huge concrete box; its façade whitewashed with rainbow trimmings. Two guards were stationed under the huge Valhalla Club logo that was fixed in bronze. Right beside them were mirrored doors that reflected the faces of customers in the neon glow of the sign atop the building. On any given night, the club's parking lot was full of cars with licence plates covered with newspaper, while uniformed guards and drivers smoked under the huge *balete* trees clustered at the lot's corner.

Once past the mirrored doors, however, the customer would find himself in a different world. The Valhalla Club appeared true to its name. Rows of long, wooden tables stretched into the shadows of immense stone walls. The customer would then be approached by one of the slender, blue-eyed Valkyries, who with a whisper of 'Welcome, *einheri*,' would lead him to his table. There, the newly christened warrior could subject himself to the full pleasures of Valhalla, drinking from horns always filled to the brim with mead and eating endless servings of boar dishes prepared in the most delectable ways. Ranging from medallions of boar with foie gras to exotic boar curries, every dish was served by the Valkyries. They also took care to refill each customer's drinking horn while providing an attentive ear to the lonely *einherjar*. If a customer wanted to become more intimate with one of the Valkyries, special rooms were located at the sides of the hall.

It is said that to be a Valkyrie at the Valhalla Club, one had to be a virgin. As such, it was rumoured that a generous compensation package awaited the Valkyries who followed a customer into the special rooms. Despite all this, it should be noted that the Valhalla Club was never raided in its years of operation—something attributed to the effectiveness with which Ericsson Chua, its owner, ran the nightclub.

Right until his disappearance during the burning of the Valhalla Club, Ericsson kept a low profile, despite his rumoured ties to influential politicians, businessmen, and even members of the diplomatic corps. He was but a shadow in the club, only occasionally seen outside his office.

Ericsson Chua was born in early 1953 to Chinese immigrants. His parents originally came from a small town in the province of Fujian. Because of a land dispute between their families, the young couple decided to elope, somehow finding their way aboard a ship bound for Manila, where they arrived in September 1951. The Chua couple eagerly settled in the sizable Chinese community in Binondo while pondering ways in which they could prosper. After a few unsuccessful business attempts, Ericsson's father decided to open a *panciteria*, taking the name of a popular jazz song for the eatery.

In those days Dizzy Malone's 'Dreaming Valhalla' was a jukebox favourite. In the same manner, the Panciteria Valhalla, which operated inside the Chua house, became successful, with *Manileños* quickly falling in love with the eatery's special *mami, miki,* and *lomi.*

The success of the Panciteria Valhalla ensured that by 15 April 1953, the day Ericsson Chua was born, the Chua family was among the Chinese middle class. To celebrate the birth of his son, Ericsson's father served free bowls of mami to the panciteria's customers that day.

The actual entry of Ericsson Chua into the world was not exactly memorable. He was born at 3.00 a.m. in his parents' house. The baby was not named immediately. In fact, Ericsson was a name suggested by one of the panciteria's regular patrons—a history student from the University of Santo Tomas. The Chuas liked the sound of the name although they were barely able to pronounce it. In this manner, Ericsson Chua only came to exist a week after he was born.

Ericsson's early childhood was spent amid the sights and smells of the panciteria, where he crawled, stood, and finally walked among the servers and customers, sometimes upsetting an order or two. By his fifth birthday, Ericsson's parents decided to send him to school.

A few blocks from the Panciteria Valhalla was a Chinese school run by Jesuits, who were chased out of China upon the Communists' assumption of power. The school was housed in a three-storey building with huge wooden doors. It had two areas: elementary classes were held in the west wing, while high school students crowded the eastern wing. Today it is part of a warehouse, but the school was once famous for its emphasis on mathematics and science. Classes were taught mostly in English, with special lessons on Chinese language and composition, as well as basic Filipino.

Ericsson was enrolled from 1959–70. Those who remembered him generally had a picture of a quiet boy who excelled in his studies but was notorious for some reason.

Though he did not graduate valedictorian or salutatorian, Ericsson maintained an average of ninety-three throughout his elementary years. His discipline record was spotless, save for an incident that happened on 13 February 1964.

Ericsson had been in the fifth grade then. Not counting his high grades and aversion to competitive sports, he tended to blend into the background. Perhaps it was this anonymity that drew Robertson Co to pick on him. Records show that Robertson Co was also enrolled in the fifth grade then. Robertson was considered problematic, with barely passing grades and a number of disciplinary cases to his name. On 13 February, right after the lunch bell had sounded, Robertson approached Ericsson. He started by telling Ericsson that he knew that Ericsson's parents owned the Panciteria Valhalla. He demanded that Ericsson give him a free bowl of miki that afternoon. Ericsson appeared taken aback. However, after a few moments, he shrugged his shoulders non-committally and proceeded down the stairs. This upset Robertson, who rushed behind Ericsson and pushed him against the railing. He then tried to strangle Ericsson.

The scene that followed was described by the disciplinary report as 'unfortunate and strange', especially since 'Mr Chua acted in a way not just out of character but also detrimental to the ideals and good name of the school.' Ericsson never did give Robertson a chance to strangle him. Turning around quickly, he gouged Roberston's eyes, then 'kicked his genitals, after which he pushed him face first down the stairs'. He then 'went up to Mr Co, who was already starting to bleed, and rammed his head repeatedly against the wall until they were separated by nearby students and teachers'. While Robertson was brought to the hospital, Ericsson was brought to the principal's office. After being orally reprimanded, he was given a two-day suspension. Interestingly enough, Robertson did not sustain any injuries. Despite being unconscious and bleeding while being brought to the hospital, he did not even have a bruise upon his admission, which led the doctors to question if a fight had indeed taken place.

It is uncertain what Ericsson did during his suspension. Though some said he stayed in his room, there were rumours that he was expelled from the Chua household for the duration of the two days. Those who whispered rumours said that Ericsson stayed in the Chinese cemetery during this time, living on grave offerings and stray cats. Whatever the truth may have been, when Ericsson returned from his suspension, those who knew him began to treat him with a detached respect that bordered on fear.

Aside from that incident, nothing of note happened during Ericsson's elementary years. He graduated with honours on 29 March 1966. In June of that year, Ericsson entered his school's eastern wing.

While Ericsson suddenly became taller and his voice changed during this time, he still avoided sports and did well in class. For the first few months of high school, Ericsson was wont to spend his breaks sitting on an otherwise empty bench, aloof to his classmates and teachers as he stared into space.

At home, the Chua family was bent on expanding the panciteria, which was generally full at every mealtime. Their clientele was also becoming more diverse, with even an occasional *probinsyano* making an appearance on weekends and holidays. Additionally, the Chuas also talked about getting a new house. As such, money was becoming an important part of family discussions.

Around this time, comic books were popular among teenagers. While local titles such as *Darna*, *Captain Barbell*, and *Lastikman* were eagerly followed, Ericsson wanted to amass a collection of American comics, especially those featuring Superman, Spiderman, and the Avengers. However, he could buy only one comic book per month with his allowance and with his family's investments right around the corner, asking for more money from his parents was useless. As such, it would hardly seem surprising that around October 1966, Ericsson decided to go into business.

By then, some of his schoolmates had begun smoking. Every day, after the last bell had rung, some students would hide behind the school building to smoke and chat. American brands such as Winston, Camel, and Marlboro were popular among these circles. However, newer, cheaper brands such as Ericsson's Asgard were always welcome.

Where Ericsson got his Asgard cigarettes has never been known. There were rumours that they were homemade in the Chua's panciteria. Each stick was an uneven piece of yellowed paper rolled in various sizes. The filters came in different colours and sizes with the Asgard name stencilled on each. Asgards came in small cardboard boxes that had stickers of a bearded Thor on them. The god of thunder and lightning was shown smoking a cigarette while leaning on his fiery goat cart, his trademark glove and hammer casually lying on the floor. Some pointed out that, coincidentally, Thor was also one of Ericsson Chua's favourite Avengers. Often, the stickers appeared browned and curled, especially during the hotter days of the year.

However crude the Asgard cigarettes may have appeared to be, students quickly bought Ericsson's entire stock. Their flavour was described as addictively nutty with a taste of honey that lingered a few seconds after their gold-tainted smoke was exhaled. Students usually finished a pack within hours, which was good considering that the cigarettes appeared to work for only a limited time. This meant that those who bought a pack of Asgards intending to smoke them later, usually found bits of wax and string where the cigarettes were supposed to be.

With the growing number of students finding their Asgards useless being added to those who had already developed a taste for them, it was no surprise that people were always looking for Ericsson. However, these people had a hard time finding him. While Ericsson still attended class regularly, he was never seen during breaks. Those who tried to confront him during class hours were ignored.

On 14 January 1967, right after dismissal time, Ericsson had been seen outside the school. He was talking to an old Chinese lady. A few of those looking for him drew near. Ericsson did not acknowledge their presence and gradually, their numbers grew. After a few minutes, Ericsson turned to face them. Without giving them time to speak, he pointed to the old Chinese lady, telling them to direct any questions or concerns to his cousin Socorro.

Though she had opened her toothless mouth, not a sound passed between the old lady's lips. People drew closer to her. It soon became apparent that she was not going to speak. Frustrated at being hoodwinked, the people then turned towards Ericsson.

Shouts and curses had been hurled at Ericsson. There was even a boy who threatened to have him castrated. Suddenly, one of the boys lunged at him. However, before he could reach Ericsson, the old lady got in his way, and the boy fell to the ground. Others tried to push their way past the old lady. But she did not budge. A few bystanders broke off everything, and by the time things were in order, both Ericsson and the old Chinese lady had disappeared.

The identity of the old lady has never been established. The existence of an actual 'cousin Socorro' is questionable, since the Chua couple had no known relatives in the Philippines during this time. Nevertheless, while the incident earned Ericsson enemies, it also attracted people to him.

Most notable of those whose attentions Ericsson attracted were members of 'the group'—a clique composed mostly of the rich, spoiled sons of influential Binondo families. A common characteristic of its members was that none of them would accept things not being done their way. As such, it is uncertain how the members got along. Membership was by invitation only, and there were rumours that a vow of secrecy and a blood compact were prerequisites for initiation. This vow appears to be eternally binding, as the surviving members all refused to be interviewed about internal group dynamics as well as the extent of Ericsson Chua's involvement in their activities. However, it appears that Ericsson held an important position within the group's hierarchy, since they met frequently at the Panciteria Valhalla.

While little can be written about the internal workings of the group, the actions of the group have become a part of Binondo lore. For example, versions of the events of 27 September 1968 can still be heard among the current student population of Binondo's different schools.

According to all accounts, at around 3.00 p.m., known members of the group had been seen in the vicinity of the abandoned Athena Drugstore building on P. Damaso. Each dragged huge, wolf-like dogs by thick chains. Although all the dogs were vicious, Ericsson's was the biggest and most terrifying.

Eyewitnesses described the dogs as ravenous, with spittle dribbling down their huge jaws. Ericsson's dog had been foaming at the mouth. A cooked ham—one of the lesser-known specialties of the panciteria—was then brought out, and the dogs were left to fight over it among themselves.

As the members of the group had stood by, the dogs had torn at each other's throats. Although it was a terrible battle,

Ericsson's dog was the most vicious. By the end of the hour, all the other dogs were dead, their exposed entrails steaming in the afternoon heat.

Despite a city ordinance against dog fighting, the viciousness of the dogs had ensured that no official of the local government considered interfering. That the members of the group were scions of the Binondo elite also proved detrimental to the local government's implementation of its rules.

The origin of the dogs has never been adequately established, yet several rumours about an underground source for what have been called hellhounds has been a Binondo urban legend since the late 1960s. Aside from its initial appearance, Ericsson's dog was never publicly seen again. However, according to those familiar with the Valhalla Club's inner workings, Ericsson was occasionally seen with a vicious-looking dog that ate from a pail of human hands. The hands, they said, could be attributed to Ericsson's links with the public mortuary.

At any rate, that incident marked the beginning of a series of activities attributed to the group. Aside from well-known incidents such as the Pussycat Orgy and the spread of cherub dust, the group was also purportedly linked to several smaller incidents. It would only be fair, however, to point out that the police were said to have arrested group members on a few occasions, but the records of these arrests would always disappear as soon as they were filed, and the group member would be free to go to school the following day. This was also true of the discipline records of group members, which were spotless through out each member's high school education.

As a consequence, it was difficult to tell the difference between an ordinary student and a group member.

By December 1969, the Chua family had moved into a two-storey house along Patola Road. The family's living quarters inside the panciteria were converted into an additional dining room, marking the first of many renovations to the Panciteria Valhalla, which by that time had become a Binondo institution. As such, when Ericsson graduated from high school with honours on 20 March 1970, the panciteria had satisfied the hunger of many famous personalities, such as Pedro Adigue, Carina Afable, and Pilita Corrales. Even President Marcos was said to have been a customer, occasionally stopping by to savour Valhalla's version of *pinakbet* with a side dish of *bihon*.

After they graduated from high school, the different members of the group parted ways. Some decided to go to college, either in the country's top universities or abroad, while others decided to become immediately involved in their family businesses. Ericsson decided to study in the United States. Although his SAT scores were remarkably high, he decided to forego the opportunity to study in universities such as Harvard, Yale, or Princeton, choosing instead to go to the University of Northeastern Indiana, from where he matriculated on 10 September 1970.

Not much can be gathered from Ericsson's stay in the University of Northeastern Indiana—a cluster of nondescript buildings situated in a sparsely populated area, a hundred miles from Indianapolis. Like most other foreign students, Ericsson lived in the co-ed Hench Hall, a dormitory on the eastern side of the campus. Because of the university's small foreign student population, the residents of Hench Hall during Ericsson Chua's freshman year were limited to one student each from the countries of Turkey, Czechoslovakia, Trinidad and Tobago, Bolivia, South Korea, and in Ericsson's case, the Philippines. Thus, membership in the University of Northeastern Indiana Foreign Students Association (UNEIFSA) during this time only amounted to eight people.

On 12 June 1974, Ericsson graduated magna cum laude with a bachelor's degree in business management and minors in history and mathematics. His college years were unremarkable for a bright foreign student save for his relationship with the student from Trinidad and Tobago.

At the onset of his junior year in September 1972, Ericsson moved out of Hench Hall to rent an off-campus cottage. There, he lived with Samantha Manning, the student from Trinidad and Tobago. Although they were often seen in each other's company, no one expected Ericsson Chua and Samantha Manning to be on intimate terms. As ranking members of the UNEIFSA, that the two were often seen together was no surprise, especially since the foreign student population had recently risen to fifteen students. Besides, it was hard to picture Samantha as anyone's love interest. Samantha was a humongous, fat woman with bad skin, frizzy hair, tiny, irregular teeth, and an abrasive attitude. As such, it was only in later stages that her pregnancy was noticed, as people initially attributed her increase in girth to her robust appetite.

Because of their relative seclusion in the cottage, not much is known about the domestic life of Ericsson and Samantha. However, it is well known that Samantha gave birth in the middle of December 1972, a couple of days before Christmas vacation began. Owing to the fact that neither the local hospital nor any public place had any records of Samantha giving birth, it can be assumed that she gave birth inside the cottage. At any rate, people were shocked when they saw the offspring of Ericsson Chua and Samantha Manning.

Among all the other mysteries surrounding Ericsson, the known details about his two children are, perhaps, the hardest to comprehend. A boy and girl, Ericsson's twins have been described as monstrously ugly. In contrast to the gargantuan proportions of his mother, the boy was a small, skeletal thing with serpentine features. If the boy had not been born with teeth, it seemed that he had started growing them within days of his birth as, according to all accounts, rows of jagged, fang-like teeth could be seen in his mouth. While toothless, the girl was by no means ordinary. Unusually pale, she appeared to be perpetually frowning and devoid of any emotion.

While no harm came to Ericsson, Samantha, or their brood, this did not mean there were no rumours about them. Some said that the twins were manifestations of evil spirits. Others said that the children's ugliness was a form of divine punishment, while some of the more ignorant claimed that they were the result of their parents' inadequate Third World nutrition.

Whatever the case may have been, it is known that upon his graduation in June 1974, Ericsson left Samantha and the twins behind to return to Manila. His parents asked that he help in the operations of the panciteria. Since his parents were traditional Chinese, Ericsson seemed to have kept his relations with Samantha and his fatherhood from them, choosing instead to leave his quasi-family behind in Indiana. Although from later events, it is apparent that some kind of correspondence was maintained after he left.

The Panciteria Valhalla had expanded during Ericsson's years in Indiana. The martial law years had proved to be profitable for the Chua family. As the president's favourite eatery, the panciteria now occupied a three-storey building and had played host to a number of visiting dignitaries such as Ugandan President Idi Amin, then American Vice President Gerald Ford, and Persia's Shah Mohammad Reza Pahlavi. Its menu had grown to include dishes with ingredients such as truffles and Kobe beef. Additionally, the panciteria also employed the services of Chua Yun Ting, a blind Chinese noodle master from the mainland, who was said to be a distant cousin of Ericsson's mother.

Despite his blindness, it is said that the noodles of Chua Yun Ting were the finest anywhere, even in China. Blinded in his forties by an accident, Chua Yun Ting could still prepare and slice noodle dough with precision while creating dishes that never failed to amaze. Ranging from soft, clay-roasted duck on a bed of noodles to his version of birthday noodles with prawns and abalone, Chua Yun Ting's cooking skills, coupled with his gentle nature, made him the most loved among the Panciteria Valhalla staff.

The Panciteria Valhalla's success ensured that when Ericsson arrived from Indiana to work as the panciteria's assistant manager, he had no difficulty re-establishing contact with the other members of the group, who had remained loyal patrons during his absence. By this time, most of his friends were executives in their family corporations.

And so, when Ericsson came back to Manila on 20 June 1974, he found himself in very good company.

Besides his friends from the group, his job as the panciteria's assistant manager brought him in contact with a variety of famous personalities. Ericsson was often the one who entertained high-level politicians and movie stars after the Chua couple first welcomed them. This was mostly due to practical reasons—Ericsson's command over both English and Tagalog was impeccable, and he was knowledgeable about a variety of topics that would make for interesting conversation. While this resulted in many invitations to social events, Ericsson would always beg off for one reason or another. The reasons for this have never been established.

Aside from entertaining the panciteria's guests, Ericsson's duties also involved marketing. However, since the Panciteria Valhalla was already well established, Ericsson's fulfilment of his marketing duties mainly consisted of buying ad space in Manila guidebooks, and occasionally inviting food critics from the country's different broadsheets.

However, on 20 August 1979, life changed for Ericsson. His father suddenly died of a stroke. Given the prominence of the Panciteria Valhalla, it should hardly be surprising that the wake and funeral were grand. Although the president was only at the wake for a few minutes, he did offer a huge funeral wreath in addition to sending across a personal representative to the funeral.

Understandably, things changed after the death of Ericsson's father. His mother was now the sole proprietor and manager of the Panciteria Valhalla, and Ericsson's duties were expanded to include operations. This marked the beginning of several changes in the panciteria.

One of the first changes that Ericsson instituted was to keep the panciteria open for twenty-four hours. The Panciteria Valhalla's prominence had made demand for its food unusually high. Customers were known to queue outside the panciteria until closing time approached. Ericsson's move made certain that the appetites of the panciteria's customers would always be satisfied. Ericsson also tried to accommodate the panciteria's customers by adding two additional floors to serve as dining rooms, in addition to purchasing an empty lot along Katapatan Road that was to be the site of the second Panciteria Valhalla branch.

Ericsson also expanded the panciteria's products. Working with Chua Yun Ting, he added several dishes to the menu such as baked quail on thin cellophane noodles, flame roasted mutton on a spit, and liquid-less turtle soup, which instantly became a bestseller as well as a novelty. Ericsson also added alcoholic beverages, stocking wines, liquors, and beers from around the world. More importantly, in December 1979, the panciteria became the first establishment in the Philippines to offer mead.

Much has been said about the mead served in the Panciteria Valhalla—a golden concoction that amazed even those from Poland and the Scandinavian countries. It is said that a sip would bring solace to the broke, comfort to the stressed, and laughter to the heartbroken. However not everyone was impressed by the new drink. There were rumours that Valhalla's mead was nothing more than adulterated beer laced with endorphins, while some said that the mead was manufactured in a dirty, old warehouse by scruffy men who would occasionally spit into the brew to add foam. Whatever the case, Valhalla's mead was ordered with most meals in the panciteria.

Ericsson Chua's changes were approved by his mother, who delighted in the revenue increases that these brought.

However, on 4 November 1982, Ericsson proposed and pushed for an idea that would affect the relationship between mother and son.

Shortly after a trip to Olongapo, Ericsson Chua suggested to his mother that the panciteria staff be replaced by scantily clad waitresses. He pointed out that this would add to the panciteria's ability to attract customers. Such a move would give the panciteria a fresh new look, especially since it would be hard to argue with the selling power of sex. Ericsson's suggestion was immediately rejected by his mother, who was appalled at the thought of replacing the staff—some of whom had been working in the Panciteria Valhalla since the mid-1950s. Moreover, she also thought that Ericsson's suggestion would destroy the image that the panciteria had spent close to thirty years building. Ericsson's suggestion led to a heated argument. By the end of the month, Ericsson Chua was effectively pushed aside when his mother told him to stop interfering with the panciteria's operations and concentrate instead on the construction of the new Panciteria Valhalla branch on Katapatan Road. They never spoke to each other again.

At this time, work on the Katapatan Road lot had not yet begun. Spanning a couple thousand square metres, the lot was enclosed by thick walls with graffiti sprayed on them. Inside, rubbish lay littered in the areas close to the walls, while a few balete trees were clustered together in the middle of the lot. After his argument with his mother, Ericsson Chua made himself scarce. There were rumours that he had left the country to go back to the United States while some said that he had begun to work in a *siopao* factory in Malabon, where he butchered stray cats for the factory's special *bola-bola pao.* Whatever the case, Ericsson Chua disappeared, only reappearing after the death of his mother on her birthday, 10 April 1983.

Ericsson's mother was poisoned at her birthday party. In a departure from traditional Chinese practice, she had eaten a bowl of birthday noodles, first and alone. To the horror of her guests, moments later, she fell face-first on to the dining table, turning purple while frothing at the mouth. Analysis later revealed that she had been poisoned by the birthday noodles, which had been laced with a complex toxic substance. Consequently, the blind noodle master Chua Yun Ting was arrested and charged with the murder of his employer and distant cousin.

During the trial of Chua Yun Ting, prosecutors found it hard to establish a motive. Ericsson's mother was loved and respected by the panciteria staff, and Chua Yun Ting was no exception. In fact, the relationship between the blind noodle master and his deceased employer appeared to be very close. During the trial, Chua Yun Ting admitted to preparing the fatal noodles, which had been requested by the birthday celebrant for her banquet. He denied poisoning his distant cousin, maintaining that he had prepared the noodles to give the birthday celebrant a delight that was by no means supposed to be fatal. Interestingly enough, those present during the trial say that Chua Yun Ting had claimed that Ericsson Chua had assisted by handing him the spices used to flavour the fatal dish. Given the old noodle master's blindness and the fact that nobody had seen Ericsson in almost a year, Chua Yun Ting's statements were not taken seriously, and he was sentenced to death, dying on the electric chair on 12 June 1984. It should be noted, however, that the name of Ericsson Chua does not appear in any of the trial's official proceedings.

Following the death of Ericsson Chua's mother, the Panciteria Valhalla closed for the first time in years. Ericsson Chua, who for years had been expected to continue his parents' legacy, was nowhere to be found. It was only on 15 December 1984 that Ericsson resurfaced and the Panciteria Valhalla reopened.

The Panciteria Valhalla reopened to only mediocre success. Since it had been closed for more than a year, a lot of the panciteria's former patrons had found other places to eat. Additionally, most of the eatery's old staff had found other jobs or refused to work for Ericsson Chua, out of loyalty to his mother. The panciteria itself was beginning to deteriorate as the floors and tables—untouched since Ericsson's arrival from Indiana a decade ago—began to creak and groan. As such, customers were greeted by creaky old furniture, bad service, and bland food. It was clear that the Panciteria Valhalla would gradually slip into obscurity if nothing was done.

Nothing was done by Ericsson to save the Panciteria Valhalla, which, after whetting the appetites of presidents, foreign dignitaries, and ordinary people for more than thirty years, quietly closed on 6 April 1985. The Panciteria Valhalla's gradual decline and eventual closure did not mean that Ericsson Chua was idle after his reappearance. On the contrary, it seemed that he was busy developing the Katapatan Road lot that was originally envisioned to be the second branch of the panciteria.

During the time of the panciteria's decline, a flurry of activity could be seen at the lot. A portion of the wall had been torn down, and several guards were posted at the newly made entrance. Every day, workmen and their heavy machines could be seen entering and leaving the lot. Some of the balete trees from the middle of the lot were also transplanted closer to the wall. As the months passed, the wall was eventually torn down, revealing a huge whitewashed concrete building with rainbow trimmings and mirrored doors, beside which was the bronze Valhalla Club sign.

And so, on 5 January 1986, nine months after the Panciteria Valhalla closed, the Valhalla Club opened. Many famous personalities graced the club's opening, among them General Fidel Ramos, Minister Juan Ponce Enrile, General Fabian Ver, and Bongbong Marcos. It would be the last time these personalities partied together before Ramos and Enrile broke ties with the government. Foreign dignitaries and Ericsson Chua's friends from the group— who by now had begun running their respective family corporations—were also present at the event, where they were all named einherjar for the first time by the beautiful, blue-eyed Valkyries.

The opening of the Valhalla Club also earned Ericsson enemies that pushed for its closure on moral grounds. Letters were published in newspapers that hit the nightclub as symptomatic of the decay of the Filipino people while priests warned their congregations never to set foot in that house of sin.

The outbreak of the Edsa Revolution on 22 February 1986 drew attention away from the Valhalla Club, although there were those who, upon the inauguration of Corazon Aquino as the country's eleventh president, thought that the club would be closed because of its links to the Marcos regime. Needless to say, no such closure happened, and despite the political changes, nothing at the Valhalla Club changed. Every night, its mirrored doors would bring in its high-profile guests to be welcomed and entertained by the lovely, mysterious, and eternally virginal, blue-eyed Valkyries.

There is a lot of debate about where Ericsson Chua got the Valkyries. Some whispered that he had shady partners in the USSR who would supply women from such places as Kiev, Leningrad, and Moscow. Others even said that the Valkyries were *aetas* that took an entirely different form inside the club because of drugs or witchcraft. The more paranoid even said that Ericsson Chua had a two-decade-old agreement with some American soldiers stationed at Clark and Subic to spread their blond and blue-eyed genes among the locals to create illegitimate children who would go on to work at the Valhalla Club.

Whatever the case, the Valhalla Club's Valkyries were seemingly infinite. No Valkyrie was ever seen in the club more than once, although the names of Brunhild, Hilde, and Sigrun were always present, albeit belonging to different faces. The einherjar seemed not to really mind this, as each sultry Valkyrie seemed to know their customer's deepest desires. In fact, it would seem that conversations with Valkyries were seamlessly carried over from one visit to the next, with new Valkyries knowing everything about their einherjar—who also found solace in the seemingly limitless mead and boar dishes offered at the Valhalla Club.

Although it seemed that the mead served at the Valhalla Club was a carryover from the panciteria days, those who had tried both swore that they were different. While the panciteria's mead relaxed and consoled, it is said that the mead served at the Valhalla Club blocked all thoughts of the outside world. Wives, children, meetings, and court cases were all forgotten with a sip, allowing each einheri to concentrate on Valhalla's delights. The never-ending variety of boar dishes, too, were said to possess the power to open senses that went beyond tasting, touching, seeing, hearing, and smelling. For the Club's Muslim einherjar—such as Arab dignitaries—*halal* mutton was used instead, although those who had tried both said that dishes prepared with boar seemed to unlock more hidden senses.

While the einherjar lost themselves in the company of the Valkyries, Ericsson Chua was usually in his office. Those who entered the office described it as nothing really remarkable save the occasional scent of dead snakes and muriatic acid–burned flesh and the occasional presence of a vicious dog in the corner of the room.

As the years passed, it seemed that the Valhalla Club remained oddly constant. This is interesting, since along with the nightly Valkyrie changes, the arrangement of the hall also seemed to change every night. Though the long tables always looked different, as did the different decorations on the stone walls, these changes always seemed to be variations of the same services that the einherjar could undoubtedly count on, even amid the chaos of the RAM coup attempts of the late 1980s.

However, between the evening of 1 June and the early hours of 2 June 1992, everything came to an end at the Valhalla Club. Those present on that night said that even before entering the club, something seemed wrong. The huge balete trees at the corner of the club's lot—which had been placed there since the Valhalla Club's construction—had been cut, leaving behind their withered roots. The rainbow trimmings of the building's façade also appeared dull and cracked. Inside, it was chillier than usual. Nonetheless, the Valhalla Club's einherjar, the politicians, diplomats, and taipans who were members of Ericsson's group, were present, entertained by the Valkyries, whose charms they could not resist despite noticing that all their fingernails seemed to be gone.

By nightfall, everything seemed normal. Families and the intrigues of the business and political worlds were forgotten; the einherjar were drinking mead and eating boar, and quite a few were leading their Valkyries into the private corner rooms. At around 10.30 p.m., Ericsson made an uncharacteristic appearance outside his office, followed by a young man and a young woman.

People were disturbed and appalled by the appearance of Ericsson's companions. Towering at around eight feet tall, the young man was thin and had a distinctly serpentine face. His shifty eyes seemed to look in different directions and he had rows of pointed teeth that were all fang-like. For her part, the young woman was short and had a greyish complexion. Her face was fixed in a sorrowful grimace. Ericsson and his two companions sat at the end of a sparsely occupied long table. Some said that Ericsson's shoes appeared to have been made of fingernails. When asked about the identity of Ericsson's two companions, the Valhalla Club staff replied that they had heard that these were Ericsson's children whom he had not seen in two decades. This was apparently their first time in Manila, and as such, Ericsson had much to discuss with them. However vague, this answer appeared to have satisfied the einherjar in their detached state, and nobody paid much attention to Ericsson Chua and his ugly children for most of the night.

Shortly after midnight, a series of strange and horrifying events began to take place at the Valhalla Club.

Although several contradictory details have been noticed in the accounts of survivors, it should be pointed out that the basic sequence of events appear to be generally consistent in the testimonies. At around 1.00 or 1.30 a.m., the main lights of the Valhalla Club dimmed then suddenly turned off. Already unusually cold that night, the temperature inside the club became freezing, and the einherjar could only snuggle against the Valkyries for warmth.

The usually smooth skin of the Valkyries seemed to feel a little damp and irregular, and as their eyes adjusted to the darkness, the einherjar saw that they were actually embracing corpses with their skins peeled off. Understandably, each customer recoiled in horror, especially those who were in the process of enjoying the services of the Valkyries in the private rooms. Needless to say, at this point, the desire to leave was great, and each warrior began running towards the exit.

The next few moments have been described as chaotic and surreal. As the customers tried to make their way towards the exit, Ericsson Chua remained seated. His two companions, however, could be seen in the middle of the pack of bodies rushing towards the club's doors. The tall young man began swallowing people. Survivors said that the young man's belly had expanded to unbelievable proportions after he had eaten a few people while the young woman watched passively. The door of Ericsson Chua's office then burst open as a huge, wolf-like dog ran towards the customers, foaming at the mouth. As Ericsson's dog tore off hands and feet, the Valhalla Club suddenly caught fire all around. Nobody really knows where the fire came from, but it quickly consumed everything in its path while thick smoke filled the smouldering hall.

According to all accounts, the smoke caused not only the customers but also Ericsson's dog and young companions, to choke and collapse. The young man in particular was terrifying, as he coughed out body parts on the floor before he finally stopped breathing. Interestingly enough, the accounts differ on what happened to Ericsson Chua. Some survivors said that he was swallowed by the young man who was reportedly his son. Others said that he was buried alive as the burning roof beams collapsed. It has also been said that Ericsson Chua melted into a liquid mass as he was consumed by flames.

Whatever happened to Ericsson Chua, it is true that he disappeared, and the morning of 2 June 1992 saw a lot of missing public officials, diplomats, and businessmen. The identities of all the fatalities have, to this day, not yet been established, as it is said that well-disguised actors assumed some identities and positions. What is certain, however, is that on that morning, the Valhalla Club—which, like its owner, had its roots in the small Panciteria Valhalla at the heart of Binondo—ceased to exist, and on its ruins was built the Church of the Nativity, a few years later.

A Reply to a Query

From: Fransisco Lacson <flacson@ateneo.edu>
To: Jerome Limpe <jlimpe@yahoo.com>
Date: 10 June 2003
Subject: RE: Folktale Appropriation Query

Dear Mr Limpe,

This is in reply to your email of 26 May. Unfortunately, I will be unable to meet with you in the next few months. I am on sabbatical until next June, and since I am currently moving around Latin America for a research project, I doubt if it would be logistically possible for us to schedule a face-to-face meeting any time soon.

However, since your exploratory research on 'Real World Appropriation of Transnational Folkloric Themes' is of personal interest to myself, I see no reason to believe why we could not correspond through email. In fact, I would personally prefer this, given the amount of spare time I have in between my interviews with the locals.

Looking at your initial ideas for the project, I cannot help but wonder about the aptness of some of the sources you mentioned. While it can hardly be argued that the cases of Hermes Uy and Ericsson Chua are intriguing and can be corroborated by textual and documentary sources, I think that their inclusion would serve to muddle your research question, since they seem to lean towards a real-world appropriation of the mythological, as opposed to the more secular emphasis of the folkloric. Additionally, I also doubt if you would be able to sufficiently analyse these, given your premise of using the Aarne–Thompson Classification System as an analytical tool. Although I am certain that the AT System would contain several entries that would be applicable to both cases, it would seem quite a stretch to expect these themes to fit together in a coherent structure, considering the episodic quality of long-drawn-out historical accounts and their tendency to lean towards pastiche. What I mean by this is that even if you manage to find several themes in the Uy and Chua cases, it would be hard to claim that these represent real-world appropriations, since the presence of other factors (economic, sociopolitical, etc.) in such a long time span might render the folkloric incidental.

Though I understand the personal reasons behind your selection of the Uy and Chua cases, I would suggest finding alternative sources that cover a shorter time period while indubitably appropriating transnational folklore. I am sure you will be able to find a couple of interesting incidents in the context of your ethnic group. If what you uncover may prove insufficient in proving your research question, you could always look beyond the Filipino–Chinese community, since your topic does not seem ethnically restrictive.

The reason for this suggestion (as well as my personal interest in your research project) is that (as I assume Dr Gutierrez had already told you when he referred you to me) I am no stranger to incidents that seem to appropriate the folkloric, having documented several cases of this during my own fieldwork. However, I have yet to conduct a formal study on this owing to the demands of my university duties, as well as the difficulties involved in finding a grant-giving organization willing to fund such a project. A pity, really, since these cases have cropped up in most my research projects since the late 1970s!

In response to your solicitation of a case-in-point to illustrate any suggestion I may have, and bearing in mind your promise of confidentiality, I would like to volunteer my most recent encounter with real-world appropriation ('Personal Reports from the Field #010495'), which happened in July 2001 when I was doing fieldwork in Manila for my study on 'The Transference and Transformation of Folkloric Themes from Rural to Urban Areas'. Since all my files have been encoded using Lotus Word Pro, I will furnish you a copy of my documentation at the end of this letter.

This particular case is interesting, since it tends to draw parallelisms to the cellar-of-blood and robber–bridegroom tales (AT Type 956) of which perhaps the Bluebeard folktale is best known. Additionally, it also seems to recall the trickster *kitsune* fox spirit of Japanese lore, albeit in a perverted manner, since the reported creatures seem to manipulate the desires of women for procreative purposes, in contrast to the more mischief-driven actions of the kitsune on men.

At any rate, I hope that you find the example useful. If you have any further questions, do not hesitate to contact me. I would also like to be given a hard copy of your paper once it is completed. Since I will still be gone at the end of the school year, could you leave a copy with the programme secretary? Thank you and good luck.

Best regards,
Frank

Fransisco Lacson, PhD
Associate Professor, Applied Folkloristics Programme
Second Floor, Vladimir Kierulf School of Humanities (VK-SOH) Building
Loyola Schools, Ateneo de Manila University
Katipunan Avenue, Loyola Heights
Quezon City, Philippines
Tel. No.: 63 2 789-98211
Fax No.: 63 2 789-98212
Mobile No.: 63 940 847-21312
Email: flacson@ateneo.edu

Personal Reports from the Field #010495

In July 2001 I decided to conduct the Manila leg of my fieldwork. Having already established that the *barangay* of Lazaro de Chino was a potential hotspot for data on urban faith healers, I arranged to stay in the house of Christina Garcia-Ferrer, whom I had known since our university days. Christina's house stood in a relatively quiet area not far from the Church of the Nativity and the faith healer stalls that were clustered near its premises. Perhaps because of their close proximity to the area, a substantial number of Christina's neighbours seemed to have pertinent anecdotes. As such, the bulk of my fieldwork consisted of interviews arranged with the help of Christina, who managed to tap into the networks she had built throughout her years in the barangay council.

Since I spent close to a month in Lazaro de Chino, I was able to familiarize myself with the neighbourhood and its people. Most of Christina's neighbours were certainly very friendly, with their invitations to sit with them outside their homes and chat over shots of Emperador. Through drunken conversations with them, I was able to pinpoint new leads for sources in addition to hearing vague, unverifiable rumours about the community such as the baby who was eaten by a goat, the prepubescent girl who returned a crone after disappearing for a year, and the crazy hag who would call out for the neighbourhood's teenaged girls in the middle of the night to put a deadly curse on them.

Understandably, not all of Christina's neighbours were that open and warm. There were some who seemed aloof and evasive. Such was an old woman who apparently lived with her middle-aged daughter and son-in-law a few doors from Christina's house. I never saw her during my rounds around the neighbourhood, and it was very likely that I wouldn't have known of her existence were it not for an incident that happened at the end of my first week.

In the early hours of 6 July, I was walking home from a drinking session. In contrast to other areas in Manila, Lazaro de Chino was a place where one could walk inebriated without fear of being disturbed. As such, despite the desolate atmosphere of the hour, I staggered past parked cars and closed shops with confidence. When I finally turned at the street where Christina's house stood, I noticed the outline of a figure standing in front of one of the houses.

As I drew nearer, I could see that the figure was an old woman smoking in front of an open gate. Because I knew the house belonged to a middle-aged couple of Christina's acquaintance, I assumed that she was the mother of the woman due to a certain resemblance between them. Although her back was already bent and there was scarcely any hair left on her head, the old woman wore short white shorts, and a tight pink T-shirt that revealed her sagging belly. The faint light from the streetlamps seemed to accentuate her liver spots and wrinkles as she took long drags from her cigarette and blew smoke streams out her toothless mouth. She appeared to be deep in thought and did not acknowledge my presence even when I walked past her.

Since the pilot study had showed that those belonging to older generations tended to yield more anecdotes, that morning I asked Christina about the possibility of the old woman from a few doors down becoming a respondent. Perplexed, Christina asked about who I was referring to. After listening to my description of the potential respondent, she told me not to bother with the old woman, since the family had just recently moved into the neighbourhood. However, the quickness of her reply and her uncharacteristically dismissive tone seemed to tell me that Christina knew more than what she was saying. Airing my suspicions, I appealed to our many years of friendship while reminding her that the purpose of my research was to uncover some vestige of human truth. While Christina initially sought to assuage my suspicions, my persistence gradually wore down her resolve until, exasperated, she said that she was hardly in a position to talk about the old lady. When asked why, Christina replied that it would be better if I interviewed the crone's parents. Ignoring my confused expression, Christina continued that the old lady's name was Innocencia de la Paz, and she was unlikely to have many anecdotes, since she was only nineteen years old.

Naturally, all this sounded ludicrous. It was hard to imagine that whom I had taken to be the crone's daughter and son-in-law were actually her parents, and it was even more difficult for me to swallow that such a relic was only nineteen. Barely concealing my irritation, I asked Christina what she meant.

Christina could only reply that she would try to arrange a meeting between Innocencia's parents and myself. Although the de la Paz couple had understandably been secretive about Innocencia's case, Christina felt that my experience with unexplained phenomena would allow them to open up to me. Knowing that this was the most I could get out of Christina, I asked her to try her best to convince them. Our conversation then ended on that note, with both Christina and me leaving to conduct our respective businesses.

While the old lady occupied my mind at different moments over the next few days, I continued with my data collection, despite being distracted by the incongruity of what Christina had told me, as well as the image of the crone's mismatched clothing.

On the evening of 10 July, Christina dropped by my room to inform me that the de la Paz couple had agreed to an interview. As expected, they had been apprehensive about the idea of someone outside their immediate circle becoming privy to Innocencia's problem but had relented after being informed about my experience in helping rid a small town in Bicol of what appeared to be Chinese hopping corpses.

And so, two days later, Christina accompanied me to the de la Paz house. Although I had passed by it a few times, I had never really paid much attention to it, even during the time when I had first seen the old woman.

Perhaps this was because the de la Paz house was nothing out of the ordinary. Much like the other houses in the area, it was a low-roofed bungalow with a small gate separating the house from the street. There was an early-model Zastava Yugo parked right in front of the gate. Squeezing between the gate and the Yugo, we made our presence known inside, with Christina pressing the doorbell switch while trying to avoid its exposed wires, and myself rapping on the cracked and peeling blue-painted gate. After a few moments, a lady whom I immediately recognized as the crone's alleged mother came up to open the gate and usher us into the house.

As Christina introduced me to Remedios de la Paz, we made our way past a small, untended garden and through a thin, screened metal door. Inside, there was an altar on which stood Santo Niño figures of different shapes, designs, and sizes, neatly arranged behind a pair of half-melted candles. After having made our way past the altar and through a doorway, we entered the living room. At this point, Remedios turned to ask us to sit on a battered-looking couch. She then excused herself to call her husband.

While Remedios was away, I took the opportunity to look around the living room that had several framed photographs propped up on the otherwise bare tables. Aside from the de la Paz couple's wedding photograph, and one that I took to be Innocencia's graduation portrait, the pictures appeared to be of the family in various gatherings. From the different pictures, I could see that Innocencia—apparently the couple's only child—was once a lovely, active girl. Although, with a bit of imagination it wasn't that hard to notice the similarities between the girl and the old woman who had haunted me for the better part of the week. As I regarded the pictures, Remedios returned with a man she introduced as Manolo, her husband.

Once handshakes had been extended, all of us were seated on the couch, and small talk was extinguished as the conversation soon turned to Innocencia's case. After turning on the tape recorder and indicating that I understood the matter to be a deeply sensitive family issue and that I really appreciated their willingness to meet with me, I asked the de la Paz couple about the circumstances surrounding Innocencia's predicament.

Biting her lower lip while her husband stared blankly at the floor, Remedios started by saying that everything had begun in May 1999, shortly after Innocencia's seventeenth birthday. While she proceeded to give a rather florid description of her daughter's situation before the tragedy (see tape 010495—1, side A), it was apparent that up to that point, Innocencia had been living a rather normal life. Although she had had her fair share of suitors and was known as a good volleyball player, there was nothing really extraordinary about her. She got along with her teachers and classmates and was usually willing to do her share of household chores. As for Innocencia's relationship with her parents, both Remedios and Manolo said that they got along with her well enough that she would even tell them about her suitors, which, by May 1999, included a certain Juan del Monte.

At this point, a livid countenance seemed to set into the de la Paz couple. Remedios, who had been smiling at different points while reminiscing her daughter's past, began to speak in a more subdued manner. Manolo, who had only said a few words, appeared to lose interest in the interview altogether. Since this sudden shift seemed to be connected to Juan del Monte, I interrupted Remedios' rambling monologue to ask her why his name in particular was mentioned among Innocencia's suitors.

With sudden interest, Manolo answered for his wife by saying that that Juan del Monte character was responsible for their daughter's deformity. Although they never met him, Innocencia had spoken a lot about Juan del Monte in the week leading to her disappearance. She had described him as a handsome, charming *mestizo* gentleman whose province-based family apparently owned the del Monte Corporation. Additionally, she had also told them that he was in Manila on business and had been visiting Lazaro de Chino to light a candle and offer a prayer in the Church of the Nativity for the sake of a few sick workers in the company's plantation in his province, which had not been named. From Innocencia's persistent mentioning of Juan del Monte, the de la Paz couple knew that their daughter's disposition to her new suitor was different from the way she regarded the neighbourhood boys. However, they really did not expect her to elope with del Monte by the end of the week.

As his wife passively looked on, Manolo shook his head while recounting Innocencia's sudden disappearance and how she eventually returned in her deformed state. On the afternoon of 10 May, the de la Paz couple returned home from a family friend's wedding reception. Innocencia had begged off from attending, since she said that she wasn't feeling very well, and her parents hardly expected her to even be out of the house that day. Instead, Innocencia was nowhere to be found. In her room, they found a note that said she and John-John (her pet name for del Monte) had fallen in love, and they had decided to go back to his province to get married and start a family. Although they noticed that Innocencia had curiously left behind all of her belongings, the contents of the note threw them in such a state of panic that they began to ask everyone in the barangay if they had seen Innocencia. Over the next couple of days, neither Manolo's rounds around the neighbourhood nor Remedios' frantic phone calls were fruitful, although a few of their neighbours said that over the week, they had seen Innocencia in the company of a tall, handsome mestizo who was chauffeured around in a black Mercedes sedan with heavily tinted windows and no licence plates.

While the de la Paz couple were initially hesitant to approach the authorities because they were afraid of the scandal it might cause, they soon realized that people were already talking. It escalated to the point that even those whom they had not approached during their initial search were trying to console them. As such, they filed a missing person's report with the police and consulted a lawyer about the possibility of filing kidnapping charges against Juan del Monte.

Over the next two weeks, the de la Paz couple continued to search for their daughter. Manolo took a leave of absence from his technician's job to look for details about

Juan del Monte, while Remedios tried to ask Innocencia's friends if she had told them anything in the week leading to her disappearance. Again, their combined efforts did not result in any concrete information. Manolo found out that the del Monte Corporation was not really owned by a landed mestizo family, but was instead, a multinational company with American roots. For her part, Remedios found out that Innocencia had neither met up nor spoken to her friends during that week. Despite the numerous dead ends that they were faced with, it never occurred to the de la Paz couple to stop looking for their missing daughter.

In the early hours of 25 May, the de la Paz couple were awakened by long, consecutive doorbell rings. Manolo said that as they moved through the house, towards the gate, they could hear an incomprehensible wailing coming from outside. He also added that when he peered outside to see who it was, he was shocked to see an old crone in tattered clothes pressing the doorbell.

As Manolo was speaking, I noticed that Remedios' lips were beginning to tremble and tears were starting to well in her eyes. After asking her if she was all right and being reassured that she was, I apologized to Manolo and asked him to continue. Manolo resumed by saying that he had asked the crone who she was and what she wanted and had been utterly dumbfounded when she called him daddy. Manolo then said that he had told the crone that she probably had the wrong address and politely asked her which family she was trying to visit.

To his shock and disbelief, the crone sobbed and asked him why he did not recognize her while telling Manolo that she was Innocencia. Manolo said that naturally, he had been tempted to drive the old woman away as a tasteless practical joker. However, he couldn't bring himself to do it since the crone's wailing appeared to be genuine, and she repeatedly said that she was sorry for not only running away with John-John but for also not contacting them for the past two years.

Although the crone's belief that his daughter had been missing for two years puzzled Manolo, hearing Innocencia's pet name for del Monte had alarmed him, since the de la Paz couple had never mentioned this to anyone. As such, Manolo said that he then asked the crone where he kept his chequebook—something that only he, his wife, and Innocencia knew. When the crone gave him the correct answer, Manolo had no choice but to open the gate.

Manolo said that the moment the gate was open, the crone stumbled through it and then collapsed in the garden. Her stench, filthiness, and relic-like appearance seemed to make a case for the de la Paz couple to drive the crone away. However, because of what she had told Manolo, in addition to the fact that her rags appeared to be the tattered remains of the clothes Innocencia had worn on the day she disappeared, they were faced with the terrifying possibility that their daughter had, indeed, become a crone in the two weeks that she was gone.

Manolo continued by saying that although they were unsure of what to make of the crone, they had felt that it was their humanitarian duty to at least help her. Since they couldn't just leave her lying in their garden, they decided to bring her inside the house before calling for a doctor.

While turning her over to lift her up, they noticed something strange. In one of her hands, the crone was clutching what appeared to be a decaying piece of flesh in the shape of a cord with a small knob at the end. While describing the thing as a rotting, organic yo-yo, Manolo said that although they almost vomited at the sight, they managed to dispose of it, especially since they figured it was nothing more than a piece from the internal organs of a pig or a cow.

Once they had disposed of the crone's rotting baggage, Manolo said that they carried her indoors, where they placed her on the couch. Manolo then proceeded to call a doctor, leaving Remedios, who had trained as a nurse in college but been unable to take the board exam, to clean and clothe the crone.

At this, my eyes shifted from Manolo to Remedios, who had been solemnly following my conversation with her husband. Remedios nodded, then softly said that although she had not relished the thought of looking at the crone's body, the old woman really appeared to be in need of a change of clothes and a bath. Besides, she also wanted to see if the crone's tattered clothes were really her daughter's.

Remedios trembled as she recounted undressing the crone and recognizing the tattered garments as the remains of a duster she had once bought for her daughter and accidentally slightly burned while ironing. She then tearfully said that while she found this terrifying, she was even more horrified when she saw her daughter's birthmarks on the old woman's body. Remedios said that she had screamed when she saw this, bringing a running Manolo back to the living room.

With tears already running down her face, Remedios continued that she and her husband had not known what to do or how to act in the face of this terrifying evidence.

However, they agreed that since the old woman was still unconscious and unable to answer any questions that they had, they had no way of ascertaining that she was Innocencia. As such, when the doctor arrived, they told him everything except that the old woman had claimed to be their daughter who had eloped two weeks earlier. Instead, they said that the old woman was a distant aunt of Manolo who had suddenly showed up and collapsed at their door at such an ungodly hour.

After the doctor had finished examining the crone, he told the de la Paz couple that although their aunt appeared severely exhausted, she would be all right after being placed on IV and allowed a few days of bed rest. Consequently, after the doctor returned to hook up the IV line, the de la Paz couple brought the crone to Innocencia's room, where she was allowed to rest.

Remedios said that the old woman had slept for a little over a day and that when she finally woke up, she had gone into hysterics, incoherently screaming about a baby Dominic, a mansion, monsters, and how sorry she was for the past couple of years. Although they had not understood what the crone was talking about, Remedios said that they had tried their best to calm her down, especially since they hoped to eventually get the answers they sought.

As the old lady calmed down over the next few days, the de la Paz couple said that they began to notice similarities between the crone and how they remembered their daughter, both in manners of speech and actions. Additionally, the crone seemed to be unaware of her aged state, since she groomed herself like a teenaged girl and had not understood questions about being older, even after being faced with a mirror and told to look at herself. Although they found it difficult to even play with the idea of having an old woman as a daughter, they knew that they had little choice but to accept her as such. However, despite their growing predisposition towards recognizing the crone as their nineteen-year-old daughter, the de la Paz couple said that they still found it hard to come to terms with her greatly altered appearance, as well as the incongruity and incomprehensibility of what the old woman said about the two weeks that Innocencia had gone missing. Since what the old lady told them made scant sense, the de la Paz couple said that they decided to look for a person who would be able to translate the crone's nonsensical ramblings into something more understandable.

With this, Remedios recounted that they had decided to talk to Christina, who had not only served as Innocencia's godmother, but who also knew a lot of specialized professionals who would hopefully be able to come up with answers.

Since she had only been listening this entire time, Christina appeared to have been taken aback when she heard her name mentioned. However, she nodded her head and said that she had not been much help, since all her referrals, from criminologists to psychologists to even psychics and shamans, had been unable to come up with any explanation. As such, Christina said that she saw no reason for someone specializing in transnational folklore not to step in and try to provide some sense of clarity.

While I was understandably thrown off by this, I nonetheless replied that I was unable to formulate an opinion before talking to Innocencia. I explained that although it was obvious that something out of the ordinary had happened, their story lacked data that only the crone could provide. Upon hearing this, Manolo first looked at his wife, then turned towards me to ask if I wanted to meet Innocencia. I nodded my head. This prompted both Manolo and Remedios to stand from the couch while telling me to follow them to Innocencia's room, which was located near the dining area, adjacent to the living room.

Once we were outside Innocencia's room, Manolo knocked on the door. A cracked, hoarse voice answered from inside, saying that we could enter. Despite what the de la Paz couple had told me earlier and my having seen the crone in a skimpy outfit during that first encounter, I was still a bit shocked when I entered the room.

Aside from close-up posters of Hollywood actors such as Leonardo DiCaprio and Johnny Depp that were placed on the pink walls, I could see around a half dozen teddy bears on the shelves. Additionally, an assortment of hangers and clothes were strewn around on the floor and the floral-printed bedspread. The crone was sitting in front of her dressing table mirror. Although her head only had a few strands of wire-like hair, she appeared to be going through the motions of brushing her hair, moving a brush down her scalp while seemingly unmindful of the red marks this was causing.

When the crone spotted us in the mirror, she stopped and put down her hairbrush beside the different cosmetics bottles on her dresser, turning around to face us. While the crone admonished her daddy for not telling her that they had company, Manolo introduced me as Dr Lacson, a close friend of her *Tita* Christina, who wanted to talk to her. At this, the crone stood up and approached me, extending a hand that felt like bony leather while asking me how I was doing. I replied that I was all right and added that since it was already getting late, and I still had interviews scheduled for the following day, I would be visiting her again over the course of the next couple of weeks. With Innocencia's agreement to this, both Christina and I bid our goodbyes to Innocencia and the de la Paz couple.

During the next three weeks, I regularly returned alone to the de la Paz residence after my daily data collection to conduct interviews with Innocencia. While she gave her permission for me to tape our interviews, which have all been referenced under tapes 010495—3–27, I also found it necessary to talk to her about a variety of things in order to develop a rapport while gaining insight into her context beyond what her parents had told me.

This proved to be particularly useful, especially in the latter weeks, when Innocencia started to become more accustomed to my presence and, as such, began to converse with me more openly and less formally. Although I am not certain why she began to open up to me in such a short time, I would imagine that this could be partly attributed to the fact that she hadn't had anyone to talk to. Aside from the de la Paz couple and a few of Christina's other specialist friends who had visited her during the first few months after her reappearance, Innocencia had had little contact with other people. As far as the other people in the neighbourhood were concerned, Innocencia had never returned after eloping with her mestizo suitor, and the crone who was fleetingly seen on occasion outside the de la Paz residence during the wee hours of the morning was just an eccentric aunt of Manolo's who sometimes visited her nephew's family.

While the Innocencia that emerged as a result of these sessions was understandably different from the one portrayed in my initial interview with the de la Paz couple, the data I gathered only reinforced my perception that there was nothing overly unique about her past. However, my interviews with the crone did manage to uncover a few details that helped my understanding of her predisposition and attitude.

For example, it soon became apparent that Innocencia had a tendency towards looking at things romantically. In this sense, she talked about how she had a difficult time picturing any of the neighbourhood boys as her Prince Charming despite the attention they showered on her (010495—7, Side B, 1:25–1:27) and how she felt her parents were overly ordinary and that they were always trying to shape her according to their unfulfilled aspirations for themselves (010495—5, Side A, 27:12–28:00).

Because of the latter revelation, I tried to steer a couple of conversations towards Innocencia's relationship with her parents. Despite her repeated insistence that she loved them dearly, it seemed that a certain tension existed between the de la Paz couple and their daughter. Innocencia said that she had avoided accompanying them in public despite her denial that she was embarrassed by them (010495—5, Side B, 7:54–8:03), and that she had stolen from her father's stash of cigarettes and had taught herself how to smoke as a way to make her troubles disappear only for a moment.

While contrasting her situation to that of the Prodigal Son, Innocencia also said that she did not understand the reason why her parents had kept her in the house ever since she returned (010495—9, Side A). She had not been able to contact anyone, since the only telephone in the house was kept in her parents' room, which was locked when they were away, and when she snuck out to visit her friends' homes, no one would answer her calls despite her certainty that they were inside. Additionally, Innocencia also said that she had difficulty understanding why her parents had repeatedly told her that she had aged and had even shown her mirrors, when she hardly had any wrinkles on her face, even for a girl of twenty-one. While I found this, and her repeated insistence of it being the year 2003 to be a bit delusional, I found it interesting for Innocencia to say that despite everything, she understood the shame she had caused her parents and could do nothing else but accept her present situation.

As our interviews progressed, Innocencia gradually began to unravel the circumstances behind her elopement. Due to the substantial number of sessions and the digressive nature of our interviews, I have decided to reconstruct the sequence of events into a linear narrative, which can be counterchecked with the tapes from 010495—8, Side A to 010495—23, Side B.

According to Innocencia, she first met Juan del Monte on the first Monday of May 1999. Since it was summer vacation, she was walking home from her friend's house when she narrowly avoided being hit by a black Mercedes sedan. While the car managed to stop within inches of a possible impact, Innocencia said that she had stood in front of the car for a few moments, dazed, until the back door opened and a man, who Innocencia said was the most handsome person she had ever seen, stepped out.

Aside from describing him as a mestizo version of Brad Pitt on a tall and well-muscled frame, Innocencia said that there was a distinct suaveness in the way the man stepped out of the car and walked towards her. After apologizing to her in a voice that Innocencia described as smooth and deep, the man extended a hand and introduced himself as Juan del Monte.

Innocencia said that in her giddiness, she had asked him if he was a movie star. With a laugh, he replied that he wasn't. He was nothing more than a probinsyano who had come to Manila for a couple of business meetings and to run an errand for a few of his workers at his family's plantation. del Monte explained that some workers had taken ill and had implored him to light a candle for them at the Church of the Nativity during his business trip to Manila. Doing so would really do no harm and could perhaps even improve the plantation's pineapple crop. As such, he was on his way back from the church when his car almost ran over Innocencia. After asking Innocencia for her name and shaking her hand for a second time, del Monte offered to make amends by giving her a ride home. Innocencia said since the man's sense of humour and good looks charmed her, she accepted.

In the course of the car ride to Innocencia's house, del Monte told her that he had been initially hesitant to visit the Church of the Nativity. This was because he was not used to going to church alone and was prone to loneliness whenever he worshipped by himself. Consequently, he also mentioned that although he wanted to avoid being lonely, he would be going back to the church over the next few days and that this would probably set the tone for his Manila trip. At this, Innocencia said that she had felt sad and offered to accompany him to the church during his visit, especially since it was summer vacation, and she also figured that del Monte was a decent, sensitive man. With a smile, del Monte said yes, and before Innocencia got down at her house, they agreed on a time to meet at the Church of the Nativity the following day.

Beginning that Tuesday morning, they had met every day at the gate of the Church of the Nativity. After lighting a candle and offering a prayer, they would spend the rest of the day in each other's company, since del Monte's business meetings always seemed to take place in the early morning. Innocencia described those days as simply magical and probably the happiest of her life. del Monte, whom she had taken to calling John-John because Juan seemed like such a serious name, had a knack for making her feel special when they were together.

This apparently held true even with the seemingly mundane things that they did over the week. As she went through a litany of activities, Innocencia said that whether they watched a movie, went to the mall, or just had long conversations over coffee, del Monte appeared to be so in tune with her needs and wants that he made her feel like a princess. Even though they had just met, he seemed to know her thoughts and was quick to act when she became tired, got bored, or, by the middle of the week, wanted to be held and kissed.

The way John-John held and kissed Innocencia appeared to have made a lasting impression on her, since she referred to it on several occasions during our interviews (010495—8, Side A, 5:22; 12, Side B, 15:47; 18, Side A, 45:23). While she said that she had allowed some of her local suitors to kiss her in the past, del Monte had made her feel as if they were the only people in the world during those brief moments. In this sense, Innocencia said that she felt a unique intimacy with John-John that made her secure, content, and fulfilled in his presence.

These feelings only grew stronger as the week progressed. By Innocencia's admission, she began to think of del Monte and herself as somehow destined for one another, especially considering the fateful circumstances of their initial meeting. Consequently, her mind became preoccupied with the possibilities that could constitute their linked future. This was only further complicated when John-John told Innocencia on Friday that he was returning to his province on the coming Sunday, as well as his subsequent admission that he had fallen in love with her.

Innocencia said that she had not known how to react to what John-John had told her. Although she had known that John-John's Manila trip would eventually end, and that the feelings she was developing were mutual, these things had been left unsaid, and it was quite jarring for Innocencia to hear them verbalized. In her panic, Innocencia had told John-John that she loved him too and that she could not bear the thought of losing him, especially since she felt that they had a future together. This prompted John-John to say that he felt the same way and that he had been thinking of asking her to marry him and move to his province. He had been hesitant to do so, since he knew that this was a big decision that would entail many sacrifices on her part. At this, Innocencia told John-John that she was willing to make the necessary sacrifices for them to be together and that she would gladly be his wife. While Innocencia said that this made John-John visibly elated, he emphasized that the enormity of the matter made it something that she needed to think about. With a kiss, he told her that he would not be coming the next day, as he wanted to give her time to reflect, and he would be waiting for her at their usual spot on the Sunday of his departure. After saying that he would understand if Innocencia failed to show up, John-John kissed her again, and they parted ways.

The next few hours proved to be extremely difficult for Innocencia. Although she had told John-John that she was willing to do whatever it took for them to be together, she was afraid that she might be making the wrong decision. After all, she would be leaving behind not just her parents and friends but also every vestige of her life up to that point. Innocencia said that during those times, her thoughts would repeatedly go back and forth between her parents and John-John. While she certainly did not want her parents to be angry with her and she did not relish the idea of being called a bad daughter, she felt that going away with del Monte was something she had to do. Staying back would mean being relegated to living her life according to the constraints of the community as well as her parents' wishes. In contrast, John-John seemed to offer a life of unlimited possibilities and, more importantly, happiness. Since she felt certain that she and John-John would be happy together, and that his family would be more than able to provide for their needs, Innocencia said that she eventually decided to go with him. Besides, she was also certain that her parents and friends would eventually come to terms with her decision, especially since she knew that they wanted nothing more for her except happiness and security.

And so, at their usual time on Sunday, Innocencia met up with John-John at the Church of the Nativity. She had earlier begged off from attending a luncheon wedding reception with her parents by telling them that she was feeling a little under the weather. While her parents agreed to let her stay home, she had felt a little annoyed that they made such a big fuss about her being sick that it took quite a while for them to leave the house. This only gave her enough time to scribble a hastily written note stating the reasons for her departure. When I asked her why she had neglected to bring even a change of clothes when she left, Innocencia could only reply that she was anxious of what John-John's parents would think of her outfits. She had only been placated by John-John telling her that she did not need to worry about any clothes, since that would be readily taken care of once they arrived at Hacienda del Monte.

Innocencia said that any misgivings she may have had disappeared once she saw John-John's face when they met at the church. After professing that no words could describe how he felt, John-John took her hand and led her to the awaiting Mercedes sedan.

Despite wanting to take in the scenery of the countryside en route Hacienda del Monte, Innocencia fell asleep almost as soon as they left the church. When she woke up, John-John told her that she had been asleep for around six hours, and, with a kiss on her forehead, he informed her that they were already inside the hacienda's compound.

In her description of what she saw from inside the car, Innocencia recounted her amazement at how much the hacienda resembled her imagined impressions of it. From where she sat, she could only see rows upon rows of pineapple tops stretching out as far as the moonlight allowed her to see. The only thing that seemed to stand out was the dirt road that they were travelling on, which appeared to cascade up and down towards nowhere.

After what seemed to her as an eternity of passing through thousands of rows of pineapple tops, Innocencia said that they eventually got to a concrete road that led up the driveway of a huge mansion. As the car pulled up the driveway, John-John turned to her with a smile and announced that they were home.

Once the car finally stopped, Innocencia said that John-John disembarked first. Taking her hand, he led her out the car, past the marble columns, up the steps, and through the enormous doors that led into the mansion.

While the interior of the mansion was understandably huge, Innocencia said that there was a certain intimate quality to the place. Though she had somehow expected the furniture to be of the fancy, ornate sort, the chairs and tables in the main hallway appeared to be newer and sturdier approximations of the furnishings they had back home. The similarities between the furniture in Innocencia's old and new homes further reinforced her perception that she and John-John were meant for each other, and she could think of nothing but the soundness of her decision as he led her up one side of a grand staircase and through several hallways with unmarked, indistinguishable doors.

Eventually, they stopped outside one of the doors. As John-John turned the knob, he told her that since they were not married yet, he had arranged for a temporary room for her to stay the night. He had also made arrangements for a priest to marry them the following morning.

Although Innocencia admitted to being a little overwhelmed, she said that her confusion quickly gave way to joy when the door was opened, and the lights were switched on. Despite the fact that she would only be staying there for the night, her temporary room resembled her room back home. For Innocencia, it was clear that John-John had gone through great lengths to ensure that she was comfortable, especially considering that he had not been inside her room before. Because Innocencia assumed that John-John had somehow reconstructed her room from her descriptions of it during the week they had spent together in Lazaro de Chino, she said that she could not help but be amazed by her husband-to-be's thoughtfulness and sharpness.

Of course, there were differences between the rooms that Innocencia regarded as welcome. For example, although the floral-printed bed set and the posters on the wall were different, Innocencia said that the patterns on the sheets were remarkably similar to the ones that she had unsuccessfully asked her mother to buy, and the posters in the room included angled shots of Leonardo DiCaprio and Antonio Banderas in relaxed, casual poses. Innocencia's temporary room also had a walk-in closet that was not only stocked with clothes and accessories that she knew would be perfect for her, but also had a wedding dress on a mannequin at its centre.

Describing the wedding dress as beautifully bedecked with pearls and intricate lacework, Innocencia said that she hardly knew what to say when John-John told her that it was hers. As such, even after he kissed her goodnight and took his leave by telling her that she should get some rest for their big day, Innocencia said that she lay in bed for most of the night while looking at her wedding dress through the open closet door.

When she awoke the very next morning, Innocencia said that she was already in her wedding dress. While she thought this odd, she did not discount the possibility that she had tried it on during the course of the previous night. As she stepped into the walk-in closet to look at herself in the mirror, Innocencia was startled to hear a rapping on the door, and John-John's voice calling her. After she told him to enter, Innocencia said that John-John walked in dressed in a tuxedo and joined her in the closet.

Innocencia recounted that after John-John told her that he just wanted to make sure that she was ready for their big day, he looked at her reflection in the mirror, paused, then with a kiss, told her that he was so happy because he had waited his whole life for someone as beautiful and stunning as her to come along. After informing her that their wedding would be held in the mansion's courtyard and a few of his relatives would be able to make it, John-John took her hand and led her downstairs to an open area where several people were already waiting.

Aside from a few men and a couple of girls who were apparently married to some of them, there was also a middle-aged man whose features resembled John-John's. Innocencia said that the moment the man saw them, he immediately approached, and with a warm embrace told her that he had heard so much about her from his son, who had called him every day during his visit to Manila. After a while, John-John's father took his leave to talk to the other people in the area. When she was sure that he was safely outside listening range,

Innocencia said that she had remarked to John-John that his father was warm and charming and then asked him where his mother was. John-John replied that she had died when he was still a boy. At this, Innocencia said that she realized that she actually knew very little about del Monte. However, because she was certain that she loved him, she figured that they had a lifetime to learn about one another. As Innocencia and John-John talked to each other, a man in flowing white robes who also looked a little like John-John, drew near, and after being introduced as the priest who was to marry them, announced that the ceremony was about to begin.

Although Innocencia described her wedding as simple, she said that it suited her just fine, since the weddings she had attended with her parents had always bored her. The ceremony took place in the middle of the courtyard, which was decorated with flowers and long lace ribbons throughout its perimeter. Innocencia said that as John-John's relatives looked on, the priest led them through their vows. Once the rings had been placed on their respective fingers, the priest told Innocencia and John-John that they were now married and could kiss. As they kissed, the people around them applauded, after which John-John announced that the reception was to be held in the mansion's main dining hall. Consequently, they all proceeded indoors to a large, high-ceilinged dining room where on a long, wide table was a spread of Innocencia's favourite dishes, which ranged from a simple, pesto-tossed pasta, to a *lechon* stuffed with a paella containing an assortment of seafood such as prawns, lobsters, and interestingly enough, oysters.

During the reception, Innocencia said that the guests repeatedly made their glasses clink in an effort to get

John-John and her to kiss. After everyone had finished eating, several people were asked to give congratulatory toasts to the newlyweds. Once this was over, Innocencia and John-John were asked to say a few short words.

Since she was taken by surprise, Innocencia admitted to having only half-listened to her husband's speech, which was apparently about how his lifelong search for the one he was destined for had unwittingly ended when his car almost ran over a girl during his Manila trip. While Innocencia said that she couldn't help but smile at the little bits and pieces that she managed to pick up, she had felt her heart race as John-John's speech finished, and it was her turn to speak. With barely an idea of what to say, Innocencia said that she decided to recount their love story while emphasizing the little details that had made her believe that she and John-John were fated for each other. Although she had felt her voice shake as she spoke, Innocencia said that she was happily relieved when she finished, and everyone in the room applauded her before clinking their glasses again.

Shortly after this, Innocencia said that the lights began to dim, and music began to fill the dining hall. As John-John's married relatives began to stand up with their spouses in tow, Innocencia said that her husband extended a hand and asked if he could have the pleasure of her company on the dance floor, which was on the far side of the dining hall.

As she and John-John danced at the centre of the dance floor surrounded by the other couples, Innocencia said that she had felt that everything seemed just right. In the same manner of their first kiss, she began to feel like she and

John-John were the only people on earth, and coincidentally, the music playing consisted of the same songs that she had put on when she danced by herself in her room over the past couple of years. In this sense, Innocencia said that she hardly took notice of the passage of time, until the guests started disappearing, and John-John told her that it was now time for them to retire to their room.

Although Innocencia understandably neglected to give the particularities of the consummation of her marriage to John-John, she did say that when he brought her into the master bedroom, she could hardly see a thing, as the lights were off. Additionally, she also said that she had been nervous and that though it was initially uncomfortable, she soon felt that their destiny of truly being together had been fulfilled, and she was happy.

The very next morning, Innocencia woke up to find John-John missing from what they agreed was to be his side of the bed. As she looked around the master bedroom, Innocencia admitted that she was impressed. Not only did the room have a ceiling comparable to that of the main dining hall, but it was also probably as big as Innocencia's childhood home. Moreover, although she had expected the room to be something similar to that of her parents, she was a bit surprised to see that if anything, it was an even better version of the room she had slept in during her first night in the mansion. Save for a few telltale signs of John-John's cohabitation such as his clothes and a few books on agricultural management, the whole room seemed to be full of things that Innocencia liked. There was a large projection television surrounded by stacks of DVDs of romantic movies, a stereo equipped with most, if not all, of her favourite CDs, and most amazingly, an immense walk-in closet filled with different outfits, as well as mirrors interspersed between the shelves and closet spaces.

Innocencia said that in her delight, she had gone through the contents of the closet, which seemed to be stocked with a variety of clothes that included not only outfits that she had only seen in the magazines that she occasionally read, but also exact copies of her favourite dresses. After she tried on a few dozen outfits, Innocencia said that she began to feel hungry. Almost on cue, she heard the door open, and when she checked to see who it was, she saw John-John carrying a tray of food. Seeing her, John-John explained that since he woke up early, he decided to make breakfast in bed for his new bride. Following her meal, Innocencia said that they spent the rest of the day in each other's company—watching movies, having meals, and just talking until night had fallen.

While there were expected divergences, an interesting pattern began to emerge in the days and months that allegedly followed. Innocencia said that she would have breakfast after she woke up, which she would take either with John-John in one of the smaller dining rooms downstairs or in bed during the times when her husband would bring it to her. After eating, she and John-John would spend the rest of the day together, enjoying the recreational equipment in their room, swimming in the mansion's pool or even just walking around the gardens. Although her new father-in-law would occasionally drop by from his retirement cottage, somewhere in the hacienda's grounds, to join them for a meal, there was hardly anyone else who seemed to be a regular fixture in the mansion. Since Innocencia initially expected that the mansion would have hosts of uniformed maids, she had asked del Monte who cooked their meals and kept the house clean, and her husband had replied by saying that although they did not believe in keeping maids since their family was 'Americanized', the wives of the plantation workers who had been trained by his late mother in cooking and cleaning would visit the mansion to help around. However, he added that it was also unlikely that Innocencia would ever see these workers' wives given the size of the mansion, as well as the fact that they were shy and preferred to work without being seen.

Aside from all this, Innocencia said that there were also sporadic visits from her husband's male cousins who, interestingly enough, would always bring their new wives to spend the first night of their married lives inside the ancestral house. It was on this note that Innocencia said that John-John had told her, uncharacteristically sternly, that the only rule in the whole mansion was to never open any of the guest rooms that were occupied for the night, especially since she knew that couples needed their privacy during intimate moments. Consequently, Innocencia said that she always made a conscious effort to avoid the parts of the mansion that she knew were occupied, even during the times that John-John was out supervising the activities in the fields.

Since all this suited her just fine, Innocencia said that she became rather used to this daily pattern, which changed very little even after she learned that she was pregnant, a few months into her marriage.

Despite the discomforts of pregnancy such as the spells of nausea and vomiting during the first few months and the palpitations and decreased mobility caused by her weight gain in the latter period, Innocencia said that she still tried

to go about her daily routine. Of course, her situation had
caused her problems, but her husband's joy at the news and
subsequent efforts to spend more time with her by asking
his father to tend to the crop throughout the duration of
her pregnancy had made this bearable. In this sense, they
continued walking around the mansion, having long talks,
and even occasionally slow dancing to soft music in their
bedroom, which made Innocencia feel that everything was
just right.

According to Innocencia, she had felt her water break in
the afternoon of 9 March 2000. Because of the videos that
her teachers had made her watch in school, she had been
expecting to undergo a tremendous amount of pain over a
long period of time. However, curiously, this was not the case,
and Innocencia said that while she had felt a sudden rush
of pain, her labour had gone very quickly, and in moments,
she had given birth to a baby boy. John-John was with her
throughout her whole ordeal, holding her hand and giving
words of encouragement, although Innocencia said that in
retrospect, it was strange why she did not wonder why he
had not called a doctor even if one had not been seriously
needed. However, at that time, she had considered the whole
ordeal as a testament to their matrimonial love.

Because it was the feast of Dominic Savio, and
Innocencia had not been in any serious danger, they decided
to name their son after the saint. Innocencia said that
Dominic resembled a smaller, bald version of his father,
with prominent mestizo features that underscored his status
as a del Monte.

By the next morning, Innocencia said that she had
recovered enough to walk again. Although John-John

continued to spend time with her and Dominic over the next couple of days, Innocencia said that he soon resumed his field visits, saying that he no longer had an excuse to prolong his father's temporary return from retirement.

During the times that John-John stayed at home, Innocencia said that things seemed as they were before. While she had initially worried that Dominic's arrival would somehow complicate their relationship, Innocencia said that her and John-John's activities were hardly hindered by the baby's presence. Dominic hardly ever cried, and they considered taking care of him as another thing they could do as a family. In fact, Innocencia said that she noticed that John-John seemed happiest when he kept her company as she nursed their son. He also enjoyed showing off the baby to his cousins during their occasional appearances at the mansion with their new brides.

By this time, Innocencia said that she had been living in the house for over a year, and since she learned that John-John had opted to send representatives to his out-of-town meetings ever since they got married, she urged him to end his moratorium by telling him that she had already adjusted to life in the mansion and that she and Dominic would be able to manage just fine. However, things seemed to be pretty different when John-John was away.

Understandably, Innocencia said that the routine she had become accustomed to changed during these times. Following John-John's instructions, Innocencia said that at least twenty minutes before each meal she would write down a list of the dishes that she wanted to eat and slip it inside the mansion's mailbox. This allowed the farm workers' wives to know what to prepare, and when she would go down to the dining room closest to the main staircase, the meal would always be laid out on the table. While Innocencia said that in the occasional instance when she had been unable to write down a list, she would still find the exact food she wanted in the dining room, she nevertheless always tried her best to write one down, especially since she thought that the workers' wives were bound to make mistakes sooner or later.

As the frequency and duration of John-John's business trips increased, Innocencia said that she began to look for other things to do. At that point, she had already watched all the movies in the master bedroom and memorized the order and lyrics to the songs in the CD collection. Although she had not yet exhausted the numerous outfits in the walk-in closet, she admitted that Dominic's expressionless staring as she modelled the clothes threw her off a bit. And so, during the days and weeks that her husband was gone, Innocencia said that she would keep busy by taking Dominic to explore the mansion's different rooms. Although she said that she and John-John had taken walks around the mansion grounds in the past, they only went through the hallways to get to the main areas of the house such as the garden and the swimming pool. Because of this, she said that she had been surprised when she discovered that the rooms were of different themes, which gave her more reason to move around the house exploring with Dominic.

Innocencia said that the times that John-John was gone for more than a week had been made bearable because of those rooms. Although they were only as big as the room she had slept in when she initially arrived in the mansion, the rooms had enough things to seem like self-contained worlds. In this sense, Innocencia said that she and Dominic would spend their time watching different anime DVDs or imagining that they were in a hotel in Paris in the modern Japanese and French-themed rooms or they would even have a taste of the rockstar life in the punk-themed one.

While exploring and her son's presence kept her happy, as the days went by, Innocencia said that she began to feel a bit under the weather, even during the times her husband was present. Though she was certain that enough time had passed for her to recover, a few of the weird feelings she had had shortly after her pregnancy still remained. For example, Innocencia said that when she walked, she would sometimes feel droplets run down her legs, but they were always dry when she looked at them. Additionally, she also complained that the headaches that were present during her immediate post-natal period had not only refused to go away but, instead, had continued to increase in intensity until her final night at the Hacienda del Monte.

According to Innocencia, on the eve of 25 May 2001, a series of events that was as baffling as it was horrible was put into action. Since John-John was away in Cebu as part of a week-long business trip, Innocencia had spent the bulk of the day exploring with Dominic. After spending most of the morning watching Bollywood movies in an Indian-themed room, Innocencia said that she had felt hungry, and consequently, she and Dominic went to the master bedroom where, as she was wont to do, she made a list of dishes that she placed in the mailbox.

Around half an hour later, when she was more or less certain that the workers' wives had already prepared her supper, Innocencia and Dominic proceeded to go down to their usual dining hall. On the way there, Innocencia said that she had seen two people, a man and a woman, sitting on one of the couches in the main hallway. When she approached them, she recognized the man as her husband's cousin Marcelo, who had attended their wedding and who, after greeting her, told Innocencia that he had gotten married earlier in the day and had brought his new wife to spend the night at the family's ancestral home. There was nothing unusual about this, since the occasional visits by her husband's relatives were always unannounced given the fact that the mansion's secure location inside the hacienda did not necessitate the installation of locks and doorbells. Innocencia said that she guided the couple to the closest guest room where, before closing the door, they fawned over Dominic while saying that they wished to have a baby as cute as her son.

After making sure that the newlyweds were comfortable in their room, Innocencia immediately proceeded to the dining hall, where she enjoyed a hot dinner that included rice, chicken *tinola*, and *embutido*.

During her meal, the dizziness and headaches that had plagued Innocencia for the past few months began to recur. While the pain initially began as a manageable throbbing at her temples, it gradually built up to the point that Innocencia's vision started to blur, and she had to put down her utensil in order to support the weight of her head with her hands.

It soon became apparent to Innocencia that this headache was different from the ones she had had in the past. Unlike the previous attacks which, although painful, would eventually plateau after hitting a certain level, this one appeared to intensify exponentially, to the point that Innocencia described the feeling as though her essence was being concentrated and crushed in her skull. Consequently, she knew that she needed to get help.

Since she couldn't leave Dominic by himself, Innocencia said that she had cradled him in one arm, while using her free hand to lean on the banister as she made her way upstairs. Although she remembered her husband's rule about never opening the guest rooms when they were occupied, especially while they were being used by his newlywed relatives, Innocencia staggered towards the room where she had earlier led the couple. While she respected the wishes of her husband as well as the privacy of her cousin-in-law and his bride, she figured that they would understand given the gravity of her situation. Besides, she had already been part of the family for a little more than two years, and it was not as if the newlyweds' moment of pleasure was more important than her overall well-being. As such, when she got to the occupied guest room, Innocencia said that she had knocked while blearily apologizing for the disturbance and asking for their help. When she heard no answer, Innocencia said that she had no choice but to open the door.

While it was dark in the room, Innocencia said that she could see something from the light of the hallway that she would have refused to believe had it not been in front of her. From where she stood, Innocencia could see that the newlywed bride was breathing heavily on the bed as a crone in tattered clothes stood in front of her. The crone was carrying what looked like a fleshy bowling ball that was somehow connected to the old woman through a cord that ran from the ball to between her legs. Innocencia said that as she looked closer, she saw that the ball was actually a bald, nose-less head which had what appeared to be a long, tubular tongue that was inserted into the bride's genitals.

Although she admitted that her initial reaction was to turn away and scream, Innocencia said that she first tried to shield Dominic from the sight. However, when she looked down, she saw that Dominic was gone, and in his place, was a ping-pong ball–sized head that was connected to her via a cord that went into her body through her vaginal opening, out of which trickled miniscule amounts of blood that ran down her legs. Innocencia said that as she saw the cord enlarge with something that seemed to flow from her body to the head, she came to the realization that the creatures had somehow taken her baby away from her and attached one of their own to her body. While she was terrified by this, Innocencia said that she knew she had to detach the thing from her body. As such, she said that she had pulled on the cord slowly and steadily, trying to endure the pain until it came off with, from her description, what appeared to be the placenta, and she lost consciousness.

When she awoke after an indefinite amount of time, Innocencia said that she found herself in the middle of an empty, grassy lot that she recognized as being in the outskirts of Lazaro de Chino. Although there was no trace of either the mansion or any other part of the hacienda, she saw that she was wearing the clothes she'd worn when she first eloped with John-John. She also saw that she was still holding what appeared to be the rotting, ant-covered remains of the head and its cord. After vomiting what looked like clumps of soil and grass, Innocencia said that she was so weak that she had to crawl home, and she could only remember fuzzy images and pieces of conversation revolving around her parents before she blacked out and awoke in her old room wearing her pyjamas. Curiously, Innocencia did not mention bringing the rotting remains of the head back to her house.

It was on this note that my interviews with Innocencia de la Paz ended. Over the next few days, as I made time to collate and mull over her case in between my fieldwork duties, I slowly came to the realization that I could offer no advice to the de la Paz couple. Innocencia's case was not as simple as telling those Bicolano villagers that putting bars across their doorways would effectively put an end to their *jiangshi* infestation (Personal Reports from the Field #961145).

For example, although the creatures described in Innocencia's narrative point to a variation of the cross-cultural vampiric viscera eater, the creatures' usage of the long, tubular tongue appears to have a different purpose from that of the jiangshi or even the Filipino *aswang*, which generally use theirs for extractive purposes (Albert and Chan 1995, 32). Because of the lack of literature concerning creatures similar to those described in Innocencia's case, which seem to have used their tongues to impregnate while relying on what appears to be an umbilical cord to extract sustenance from a constant victim over a protracted period, it was virtually impossible to offer an explanation to the de la Paz couple.

Additionally, despite the parallelisms inherent in the case's marital context and the mention of the unheeded warning to AT Type 956, it was apparent that nothing that could be translated into practical advice could be derived from these. If anything, the closest approximation of the case to the folkloric can be derived from the section on the kitsune found in Morano and de Lara's seminal work on Japanese folklore (1983), which describes a case where a fox spirit tricked a man into a two-week marriage that he believed to have lasted for fourteen years.

Despite the parallelisms between the tale and Innocencia's case, especially in terms of context and the perception of time, this offered neither answers nor solutions, since the man in the tale had aged and had permanently lost parts of his mental faculties when he was found. In much the same way, although Innocencia had recovered enough to recount and converse after the incident, she had been unable to accept that her son and the small head were the same entities, which would seem to be the only plausible explanation given the presence of the placenta and umbilical cord, and her constant attachment to her son after she gave birth. More seriously, it was also clear that Innocencia's denial had implications on her perception of time and herself given her continued insistence of it being two years later than it actually was, as well as her incongruent manner of dress and action. Consequently, there was nothing I could really do to help, since the physical damage appeared to be permanent, and there might be repercussions if Innocencia managed to overcome her denial. As such, right before the Manila leg of my fieldwork ended and I left Lazaro de Chino, I apologized to the de la Paz couple for not being able to provide the answers they had hoped for, while telling them that if there was any consolation, their daughter's case would hopefully serve as a reference for future occurrences of young women returning as crones after disappearing to follow what they perceived to have been their destiny.

The Life and Death of Hermes Uy

Reproduced here is most of 'The Life and Death of Hermes Uy', which is found in Rainier Chua's *Mysterious Ongpin: a Collection of Stories on Chinese Entrepreneurs* (1972. Manila: Newlife Publishing).

[A]nd if one would go down P. Damaso, past the vendors and the beggars, past the majesty of the Church of Santa Catalina, and past the car-part depository, one would surely notice the site of the first Athena Drugstore. Although boarded-up for more than a decade, the building still subtly hints of an opulent and vibrant past. Each intricate groove of the once-famous carvings on the façade is still deep; every plank-covered window still retains some of its welcoming magnificence. On rainy days, when the drains clog and the floodwaters begin to rise, one can see the drugstore in a dirty, ever-changing mirror. Frankly, there is not much difference. For all its hints of an opulent past, the building is still abandoned, decaying, and out of place. However, in the 1950s, after less than a decade of Philippine independence, the first branch of the

Athena Drugstore chain was one of the most talked-about places in Manila, mostly due to the efforts of Hermes Uy, its owner.

Born in the middle of the 1930s, Hermes was a child of the war. His father, in an attempt to flee Chang Kai Shek's purges, had migrated from Nanking, China, in the 1920s, bringing nothing but his doctorate in Classical Western Studies to an alien land. He lacked what was considered a necessity in American Manila—a good command over English. Nonetheless, he was able to marry, finding a wife from the thousands of Sangleys that occupied Manila in its post-Parian era.

However, without any university post, a doctorate in Classical Western Studies simply did not translate into money. Because of this and an already-pregnant wife, Hermes' father had to find employment in his father-in-law's furniture shop where, until the war broke out, his main job was to carve the less-intricate designs on cheaper orders.

Being a specialist in Hellenic mythology, Hermes' father chose to name his firstborn Hermes, for all the kicking in his wife's stomach reminded him of the wily messenger of the gods.

However, when Hermes Uy was born on 18 November 1935, there seemed nothing godly about him. At birth, he weighed seven pounds and had no distinguishing birthmarks. It was in this same manner that Hermes Uy's first few years were not very memorable, with his first words and steps the only recorded moments. However, this was to change with the outbreak of the Second World War.

Although the Pacific War was but a blur in young Hermes' memory, it signified the start of an important phase in his life. Hermes was barely six when war broke out. By then, he had lived a life that, save for the occasional stories from Ancient Greek mythology and the constant exposure to the smell of lacquered wood, was perfectly nondescript for a Chinese boy living in Manila. With the outbreak of war, Hermes' father, with the memories of relatives killed in the Rape of Nanking still fresh in his memory, immediately forsook his life as a minor furniture carver and volunteered to serve in the guerilla forces as a member of the Hua Chi militia. Hoping to carry the banner for the Chinese people, he left wife and son to head for the hills. However, unlike other families, whose businesses suffered greatly, Hermes and his mother did not starve throughout the scant times of the war. During the advent of his life, Hermes showed the first glimmer of his future.

In the days of the Japanese occupation, when the most basic necessities were rationed and Mickey Mouse money inflated the market, Hermes proved himself to be very resourceful. A few weeks after the Imperial Army started rationing and printing huge amounts of currency, some of those who dared venture outdoors were treated to an interesting sight.

Outside the Uy's house, people began noticing little papier-mâché figures on a little cardboard box. These were of little men, women, and animals, all in different poses, all having very distinct features. There was a Manchu emperor, flanked by an elegantly dressed courtesan beside a caged Pegasus. There was also a *barong*-clad gentleman on a *carabao*, which was being led by the Greek god Pan. Although the images were culturally and scientifically impossible, not a few people stopped and stared at the presentation with utter amazement. It wasn't that they had never seen papier-mâché figures before, and even though a lot of people had not heard about the wonders of China or the grandeur of Hellenic Greece, there were people who knew about these things who also stopped in their tracks, dumbfounded. People were drawn to these papier-mâché figures because each one was automated.

The little Manchu emperor, seated on his Imperial throne, would look up and down at his cardboard and paper realm, the contented smile on his face visible to all. In contrast, the pretty courtesan would cover her face with one of her long sleeves, now and then moving her arm to show an intricately designed face with the lips drawn in a rather demure manner. The comedy of the elegant man in a barong riding the carabao was highlighted by the man's scratching his butt as the carabao swung its mud-caked tail. However, Pan and the Pegasus were faulty in that their divinity seemed to be more nominal than anything. Pan's movements were very much unlike the carefree dancing of the demigod. They resembled a slow goat. In the same way, Hermes Uy's Pegasus was more of an old nag than anything else.

Nonetheless, the public did not seem to mind these faults and as the days passed, more and more people stopped to watch the daily performances of the papier-mâché figures. Eventually, the show caught the attention of the occupying Japanese Imperial Army.

Fearing subversive art, the Japanese dispatched several soldiers to check the shows. When the soldiers returned, they made a full report to Lieutenant General Kinhide Tanaka, who commanded Manila during the early days of the occupation. The news the soldiers gave their officer was interesting. The show apparently amused the soldiers, who all said that although they found no subversive material in the show, it would have been better if the owner would create Japanese figures as well. Lt Gen. Tanaka regarded this matter for a few silent seconds. He then spoke of the importance of winning the hearts and minds of the people. Apparently, he saw Hermes' figures as a way of gaining public support for the occupying army. He quickly sent for Hermes.

Although an ethnic Chinese, Hermes did not show any resentment towards the Japanese. He agreed to put in a grand samurai and a kabuki actor in his theatre of papier-mâché figures, with the Japanese pledging to supply them with two extra rations of food for the duration of the war. The next day, the Japanese were pleased to see a grand samurai warrior beside the barong-clad man on the carabao. With his great *katana*, the samurai would cut invisible enemies in the air. The kabuki actor never did show up. However, nobody seemed to mind, not even the Japanese, who never noticed that their samurai warrior was made out of shredded Mickey Mouse money. The Uys ate well for most of the war because of the agreement, even after the mechanical movements of the Manchu emperor finally ground to a halt.

A few months after leaving to join the guerrilla forces, Hermes' father came back home. He had been injured in one of the skirmishes that the Hua Chi unit figured in, a stray bullet shattering his kneecap. Although he resented the Japanese and all they stood for, he accepted his family's extra rations without a qualm, as he had learned on the front that hunger was more dangerous than any human enemy.

Over time, the family barely managed to satiate their starvation many times, usually under the obscure cover of anonymity. However, all this ended with the 1945 surrender of the Japanese, which in effect heralded new times for the Uy household.

His father-in-law was long dead, and the furniture business was long gone, so Hermes' father decided to ride the tide of the times. He found a job working in the US army stockrooms. He made a few friends in the US army, people who gave him the nickname of Shanghai Uy (he was from Nanking). These army friends encouraged him to smuggle and sell surplus army goods to the public, whose appetites were already whetted by the years without Coca-Cola, Hershey's, and Spam. Not surprisingly, Shanghai Uy became wealthy in the years following the war. However, finding bigger lodging and eating rich food didn't seem to be a priority for Shanghai Uy, who maintained his lifestyle with the argument that he managed to feed and shelter his family adequately and that an extravagant lifestyle would drain his newly acquired wealth.

While his father grew wealthy, Hermes moved into his teens. He did not do well in school, despite his father's PhD. By his sixteenth birthday, he had only completed a third-grade education. The odd skills that he showcased as a child seemed to have disappeared. He spent most of his time idle, the only sign of brain activity was him fiddling with the abacus his mother had given him when he was younger. Occasionally, the sharp collision of beads would be heard around the Uy household through the wee hours of the morning. Though her sleep was disturbed, Hermes' mother would wear a strange smile as she listened to the sound of clashing beads, almost as if some far-off memory was being stirred. However, Shanghai Uy the Surplus King thought differently. He usually attributed his son's distaste of school and his abacus recitals to a childhood enclosed in the smell of lacquer. The former professor of Classical Western Studies seemed to forget that it was his son's shows that kept the family full during the war. It didn't really matter though. Business was brisk. Life was good.

And so, when his father finally died of an aneurysm during the early months of 1950, Hermes found himself an heir to a sizable amount of money. Though the money was enough to live on for a while, with the mother an unskilled housewife and the son halfway to a grade school diploma, the family knew that life was not sustainable. Coupled with the fact that Hermes was still a Chinese citizen under Filipino law and therefore prohibited from professional occupations, like many other Chinese, he was forced to set up his own business.

For weeks, Hermes did not know what to do. The years of inactivity seemed to melt away as Hermes paced the small Uy house, smoking pack after pack of cigarettes as his mother worriedly watched him. One night, Hermes suddenly stopped in his tracks. He rapidly told his mother that he was going to dabble in the pharmaceutical trade. To the amazement of his mother, he presented her with detailed ideas on how to make and market placebos and how to import chemicals from Taiwan, where they still had some relatives. However, his mother's shock wore off the next day when she woke up seeing Hermes sitting down, staring into space as he moved beads on his abacus. Yet, Hermes was all but idle. As he sat, Hermes toyed with using his name on the shop's signboard. He imagined a big, opulent sign with the words 'Hermes' Drugstore—The Fastest Service in Manila' stencilled in bold colours. However, when he checked his dad's notebooks for the meaning of his name, he discovered that aside from being the messenger of the gods, Hermes was also the god of thieves. He looked at the other pages of the notebooks and saw many interesting possibilities from Zeus to Apollo to even Asklepios. Eventually, he decided on the goddess Athena, conjuring up the now-famous slogan of 'Athena Drugstore—The Wise Choice'.

With Athena Drugstore already a reality in his mind, the next few months were a flurry of activity for Hermes Uy, who tirelessly went through the bureaucracy involved in setting up a business.

On 14 March 1951, right after the mourning period was over, the first branch of Athena Drugstore opened on P. Damaso. Since Hermes had no real connections, the cream of Manila's society was understandably absent on opening day. Only his mother, a few curious people, and those enticed by the promise of a 10 per cent opening day discount bothered to drop by.

People found the early version of Athena Drugstore neat but bland. Like most drugstores, it was a one-floor place, its centrepiece a huge wooden counter with the insides hollowed out and made into a glass-covered cupboard. Different sizes of medicine bottles were put on display under the green-hued glass. During the first few weeks following opening day, the neighbourhood children would go to the store and press their hands and foreheads against the glass display case. Then, they would step a few metres back and giggle at the foggy green imprints they left. They would run out when they heard the shouts of Hermes Uy, who manned the store by himself. It seemed that these periodic episodes were the only things that gave life to Athena Drugstore, which almost broke even in the first month.

Poring over his receipts, Hermes couldn't understand why Athena Drugstore had made such a small profit. His selection was complete, his store clean, and he served his customers courteously and quickly. Seeing nothing wrong with his store, he decided to look outside his shop.

Hermes noticed the different vendors hawking their wares along the expanse of the newly asphalted avenue. He looked at their sunbaked faces and their sweat-stained *camisa de chinos* and skirts. They all sold a variety of goods. There were wicker baskets full of *ukoy*, biscuits, and *balut*. *Bilaos* of *puto* and *kutsyinta* sat beside plastic water pistols, rosaries, and candles. Each vendor had his or her own way of attracting customers. Some gesticulated in the air, drawing attention to their goods through the language of movement. Others whistled in high and low pitches, filling the air with disorganized musicality. There were even those who took to tapping the shoulders of prospective customers and then, with a big smile and a wink, offering a sliver of puto or shooting a stray cat with a water pistol. After looking at the vendors, Hermes went back into the store. He had an idea.

The next day, Athena Drugstore did not open. Instead, Hermes was seen outside the store, talking to some vendors. Their meeting was held under the oppressive heat of the April summer. There were proposals and counterproposals, ideas accepted and refuted. Finally, after three hours, the two sides reached an agreement.

Over the next few days, people passing through P. Damaso noticed something odd. Save for the ones near the Church of Santa Catalina, there were no more vendors. Absent were the gestures, sounds, and distractions that somehow gave character to the avenue. Although a lot of people were at first flabbergasted, it was not long before it became generally known that the missing vendors had begun working at Athena Drugstore.

With the introduction of the street vendors as new employees, Athena Drugstore changed. A lot of new shelves were added, for, aside from the usual chemicals and placebos, the store now began to carry a variety of different goods, some common on the street, while others, rare imports. The usual bilaos of *kakanin* were placed beside bottles of the finest balsamic vinegar. Plastic water pistols were guarded by red-coated tin soldiers. It seemed that Hermes Uy was bent on Athena Drugstore becoming a self-contained commercial centre, a place where one could inquire on the price of a *cavan* of rice while selecting the newest jazz record. As they had done in the streets, the former vendors used their methods to coax customers into buying, their shrill sounds and amusing gestures infusing the store with a bazaar-like aura. Yet, as before, Hermes would always be the one who closed the store, checking and tabulating the receipts for the day.

Not surprisingly, a lot of people began to visit the drugstore. Professionals and the unemployed, maids, doctors, and even lawyers were among the multitudes that rubbed elbows daily at Athena Drugstore. Clearly, Hermes' plan was a success. However, successful as it might have been, it was not without problems.

While the number of customers steadily grew, the store still stayed the same. In only a few weeks, what first seemed spacious began to look cramped. The vendors drowned each other's sales pitches. People increasingly found it difficult to buy what they needed. In fact, it soon became apparent that the bazaar idea would only work if the number of people remained constant at a certain level. This being said, no one was shocked when Athena Drugstore was closed on 28 January 1952 for renovations. People saw it as a minor inconvenience and, as most of them were wont to do, went elsewhere to shop.

It is hard to know about Hermes Uy's activities during the period between 28 January and 29 October 1952, when the new and improved Athena Drugstore opened. Whispered rumours, some still unburied today, were common among the curious. It was said that he was involved in a lot of shady deals during those months. Others even hinted of dealings with the occult, with night meetings and pacts sealed in blood. But in truth, no one was sure of anything. In fact, the only insight into Hermes' life during those months was an official document that sparingly told of his 10 October marriage to one Trinidad Ramos.

The relationship between Hermes and Trinidad Uy has never been clearly established. Save for occasions where Trinidad's face was veiled under the cover of darkness, they never appeared in public together. People suspected that their marriage was a sham to counteract Hermes' Chinese citizenship. Some rumour-mongers said that Trinidad was a sixty-five-year-old maid employed by Hermes, while the more malicious claimed that there was no Trinidad at all, but different women hired on different occasions to give credibility to Hermes. The Uy couple officially never had children. Nothing was proven though, and the presence of a wife in Hermes Uy's life was to be placed in the periphery, sham or real, proven or not.

On 29 October 1952, the doors of Athena Drugstore were once again opened to the public. Those who came to the opening were shocked with what they saw. Although the sidewalk vendors, with their common and exotic goods were still there, people saw that this was certainly a store that was much different from the one that tried to be the bazaar of the people.

Spanning three floors, the new Athena Drugstore seemed to be much bigger, as if it were a whole world compressed into an area only three storeys high. Aside from the numerous vendors of yesteryears, there were also a lot of new employees. It almost seemed that Hermes had been around the whole world, looking for new employees and goods over the past few months. There were Khmers with their intricate silversmithing, Chinese contortionists, British tailors who churned out bundles of tweed for people, who generally thought the material a little itchy, and even Japanese artisans who finely lacquered pieces of driftwood for their amusement. There was even a Greek merchant selling antiques, with rumours circulating of Athena's mirrored bronze shield and helmet of invisibility, as well as the tapestry woven by Arachne, being hidden among his trunks. While the first floor still looked a bit like the grand drugstore bazaar of old, with its bilaos of kakanin and red-coated British tin soldiers, the second floor was different. It seemed to be a world of dolls rather than humans.

Here, there was a theatre where porcelain-faced dolls sat up, danced, and talked, not just among themselves, but with prospective buyers too. They would each tell melancholic stories of war and separation that were not just untrue but also painful and almost credible as well. They would talk of separations from old loved-ones and the possibilities of new love stories. They would dance to nimble beats, their glass eyes somehow reflecting the pain that the listeners felt with every soft syllable spoken by the dolls. It was a weird sight, really, with grown men loving and crying over dolls, which were controlled by a puppet master in the background.

The second floor also contained a small, darkened bar, where the soft strains of jazz fluidly moved with the soft murmurs of people. The trombone player was Black, and just like the others downstairs, no one knew where Hermes Uy found him. Although the bar served the usual drinks and cocktails, there was one drink that caught one's attention. Called Bacchus' Delight, it was a gold-hued concoction that was said to contain ambrosia and nectar. With this drink, rumours ran rife that Hermes had found the secret to happiness. In fact, there were stories of sullen-faced customers who became lively and animated after drinking the house specialty.

Although people freely moved around the first two floors of the new Athena Drugstore, the third floor remained closed. There was a big, thick chain wound around the banisters of the staircase that led to the top floor. In time, people began to whisper about what was on the forbidden floor. Those who still believed that Hermes Uy had made a pact with the devil said that this was where the black Sabbath was held. Others thought it to be a *calamansi*-soaked depository for the corpses of immigration officials who had threatened to have Hermes deported, or for the Trinidads that Hermes replaced. Some even went so far as to speculate that the third floor was a gateway to a realm that had everything but was nothing in itself, a place of nil where one could procure anything out of the void.

The third floor was actually the store's stockroom, a dusty place with bales and crates labelled in scripts both familiar and indecipherable. For his part, although Hermes Uy was somewhat aware of the rumours that went around about him and his store, he paid little to no attention to quashing them. They didn't do him any real harm and were even good for business in a way.

During those times, business was truly good, and Hermes found himself making steadily rising profits. Yet, money didn't change Hermes, who still remained in control of the subtleties involved in running the drugstore. During the relatively lean hours, Hermes would remain behind the green-hued glass counter, filling prescriptions that came to him with the gusto and promptness of one still scrounging for each peso in order to survive. However, as soon as the crowd thickened, Hermes would leave his spot behind the counter and go around the store to supervise his realm. He would make his rounds through the grand bazaar, looking over the quality of his merchandise and questioning the vendors about the day's details. It seemed as if he had more than two sharp eyes, things such as loose threads and mild discolourations did not escape the web of his all-encompassing glance. After going around the bazaar, he would then head to the theatre of the dolls where, in the shadows, he would talk to the puppet master. When the whispers in the backdrop of the theatrical laughter and tears had finally fallen silent, he would usually be seen heading towards the bar. In the bar, Hermes would have a glass of Black Jade liquor and, with that done, walk back to his spot behind the counter. He would then wait for closing time, watching as each person—customer or employee—left into the night. After the last customer had left and the last employee had gone home, Hermes would start going over the receipts for the day, only finishing in the wee hours of the morning.

However, people rarely talked about the work ethic of Hermes Uy. Aside from the different rumours that periodically circulated about Hermes' evil dealings, people also put their sights on looking for minor flaws in the store, things that they considered telltale signs of an inevitable collapse. These people would point out that the store's partial nature as a bazaar made it a potential haven for pickpockets and other vagrants. The same ilk would also sneer that the theatre of dolls was a sham that played on people's love for archaic melodrama and that the presence of the jazz bar drew people away from the church. Even though the presence of these flaws was argued eloquently, there were a few things that were obviously overlooked. First, these people were not aware that ever since part of it had become an unofficial bazaar, there had been no incidents of theft in the drugstore. Unknown to most, Hermes Uy employed quite a large number of plainclothes security men who silently whisked people away at the slightest movement towards trouble. The store's detractors also overlooked that the appeal of the theatre was the raw emotion the dolls brought forth in people who considered themselves immune to emotions. In fact, some of the very same people who scorned the theatre covertly owned a few talking dolls in their homes. The comedy behind the jazz bar comment was heightened by the fact that Hermes Uy was a non-practising Buddhist.

As months, and then years passed, the store's profits grew, and accordingly, Hermes turned to medium-scale philanthropy, donating sizable amounts to groups such as the Filipino–Chinese Chamber of Commerce and Industry, the Sun Yet Sen Society, and the Hua Chi Volunteer's Fund. Though life was good, Hermes knew that things would not always go smoothly.

In November 1953, Hermes' mother, her name forever lost in the Binondo bureaucratic fires that ravaged the 1960s, died. Hermes closed the store for a week as he mourned. The wake was at the old La Funeraria Paz in Recto. Because of Hermes' philanthropy and the sheer number of the store's loyal customers, there were a lot of guests offering both flowers and condolences. In turn, while the servants rolled the fake money and listed the real kind, Hermes sat in the front pew. He was dressed in all white, his head downcast. He received guests cordially, shook their hands, exchanged a few curt words, then slunk back into his pew as a veiled Trinidad stood among the flowers at the corner of the chapel. Though she wore black and almost did not acknowledge the presence of guests, people left the wake with the eerie perception that Hermes and Trinidad were separated parts of one person.

On 24 July 1954, President Ramon Magsaysay signed R.A. 1180 into law. Also known as the Trade Nationalization Act, the bill made it illegal for foreigners to take part in the rice, rubber, and retail industries. Not surprisingly, a lot of foreign-owned businesses were badly hit. Athena Drugstore was no exception, especially since rice, rubber, and retail goods formed an integral part of the bazaar. And so, despite rising profits during the previous seasons, Athena Drugstore was once again shut down on 11 August 1954. For one whole year, the store remained closed. Through all that time, Hermes was behind the scenes, trying to drum up excitement for the latest incarnation of his shop.

In the months preceding the opening of the newest version of the drugstore, people began seeing interesting posters around Manila. In the early months, the posters depicted the Greek gods in different states of repose. There was the splendour of Zeus and Poseidon in the full majesty of their realms. The twins Apollo and Artemis were shown contemplating their lyre and bow. There was even a poster of the misshapen Hephaestos working the bellows. Yet, the poster that was by far the most popular was the one of a bare-breasted Aphrodite smiling seductively from her crib of foam. However, in the weeks leading to the actual opening of the store, a different series of posters began circulating.

While the Greek gods were once again put into focus, the new posters seemed to attempt to reach a wider audience. Where everything was once hand drawn, movie stars began popping up. It was apparent that Hermes Uy had managed to crack some sort of deal with the Vera family, who owned Sampaguita Pictures. In her usual place as the lead role, Gloria Romero posed as different incarnations of Athena. Ranging from parodies of Uncle Sam's 'I Want You' posters to more original posters showing Athena as a Pinay everywoman, the posters appealed to everyday Filipinos. There were also posters that included Marlene Dauden as Aphrodite, Susan Roces as Artemis, Mario Montenegro as Zeus, and Eddie Arenas as Hades. Like Gloria Romero's Athena, the latter posters of the other gods were mostly caricatures that tried to appeal to the masses. There was Zeus in his philandering mode, surrounding himself with lithe maidens.

There was Hades with a goofily villainous smile on his face, proclaiming to the world that Athena Drugstore was the path towards an exciting life. There was even a poster of Pan, half of his face human and handsome where he had applied Athena Drugstore face cream.

And so, when Athena Drugstore finally opened again on 11 August 1955, hundreds of people eagerly turned up. Hermes Uy's remodelling did not disappoint. While the world bazaar was greatly cramped due to R.A. 1180, the new store made sure that people would not miss the vendors and their goods.

Outside the store was a huge bronze statue of Athena with one of her hands outstretched towards an olive tree, her gift not only to the Athenians, but also to humankind. On the first floor, where half of the bazaar once stood, there was now a mini theatre that not only showed the latest films of James Dean, but also the most exciting 3D movies as well. The scaled-down bazaar sold the trendiest goods such as stateside wiffle balls, phonographs, and hair grease. Perhaps the most notable addition was a Belgian who would create caricatures of clients on small tapestries in less than an hour. There were no stairs in the whole store. Instead, Hermes Uy installed the first escalators in the country. How the excitement burned on people's faces as they rode the escalators, terror and pleasure melding into one as they saw the ground shrink right in front of their very eyes. Quite a few people fainted because of the excitement. Women shrieked. Children squealed. Men gasped.

While the escalators proved to be popular and amazing to the crowds, nothing could prepare people for what lay on the second floor of the newest incarnation of

Athena Drugstore. The theatre of the dolls was gone, the only things that hinted at its existence being a sense of melancholia and the faint smell of salty tears that still lingered in the air. In its place was a row of glass boxes filled with muddy water and framed in layers of polished brass. While the dolls were appealing because they touched and released each person's inner melancholia, the brass-trimmed boxes were much better. They bored into the recesses of each person's soul, satisfying lifelong hungers in a few rented minutes. By looking at what was reflected through the opaque muddiness, people began to satisfy dreams that were once implausible and unreachable. Some chose to blend into the darkness, twisting their beings into shadowed abstractions until they returned to nothingness. Others saw the need to transform themselves into beings of superhuman power, avenging wrongs or moving beyond the boundaries set by society. There were even those who tried to reconstruct their features into what they considered as the perfect human, not a few modelling their temporary new features after those of James Dean.

The bar remained where it was, with the same drinks and the same band, which, oddly enough, still played the same songs.

Perhaps the biggest addition to the drugstore was the opening of the previously inaccessible third floor. The stockroom was no more. It was now the Hallway of Clear Minds. There, the distraught walked around in endless circles. The rejected and the heartbroken remained withdrawn and oblivious to others, even though most thought that going to Athena Drugstore would somehow open up new paths and possibilities. The bankrupt sat in the corner, twiddling their thumbs, silently reminiscing better times. Even those without problems roamed the hall, as most found the soft lighting relaxing and pleasing to the eyes. When these people left, they always felt much better, as if they were able to sort out their minds.

As Athena Drugstore changed, so did Hermes Uy. No longer was he seen behind the green glass counter in the middle of the store. People did not know how he now spent his days. It is said that he enjoyed roaming around the drugstore in different disguises in order to find out what people wanted improved and expanded. One day, he was an old, bespectacled lady laden with jewels. The next day, he was one of the few vendors that were left in the old bazaar, a Zulu. And the day after he was a disheartened youth wandering around the Hallway of Clear Minds. It is said that on some days he liked to dress up as Trinidad, which would perhaps explain the sudden emergence of Trinidad's sightings as people began to talk about a lady whose face was either nondescript or veiled in darkness. However, Hermes still did retain some of his older habits. He still gave increasing amounts of money to charity. And even in disguise, Hermes Uy still insisted on being the last one to leave the store, only leaving after going over all the receipts for the day.

It is apparent that all the disguise-filled days of Hermes were not in vain, for, in the next few years, while a few new branches of Athena Drugstore came out in some locations such as Patola and A. Ampil, the original store began to grow bigger and more intricate.

In December 1955, without closing the store, Hermes started the first of his new improvements. He redecorated and revamped the first floor. In a move similar to his pre-reopening posters, he had workmen paint murals of the Greek gods on the walls. Now, customers could go around the shop under the watchful eyes of Poseidon quenching his thirst on an Athena Drugstore tonic or Helios applying suntan lotion. The bazaar, now a fraction of its former size, was divided into different themes. There was an Arab souk and a Chinese medicine corner; the different smells of frankincense, cloves, and rose water intoxicating customers with dreams of faraway and different places. Under the projector at the back of the theatre, a strange box with indecipherable inscriptions etched on its lid was placed. Upon receiving their 3D glasses, each moviegoer was hooked to the box via a special apparatus that was strapped to their torsos. As the movie started, and things started jumping off the screen, people had an experience of the fourth dimension, the sensations they felt being a flurry of something beyond description in the limits of the three dimensions.

From this starting point until 14 April 1957, Athena Drugstore underwent a series of interesting changes. New annexes and extensions were built. Some proved man's mastery over the tools that allowed him to move beyond his normal capabilities. These included a machine that allowed one to understand all the subtleties involved in each sentence uttered and a room that allowed people to see and actually experience their dreams, the pain real, the wounds fresh. Other rooms, such as the one-way portal to unknown places, failed to generate any income. The huge Athena statue changed a few times as well, with a depiction of Athena's birth from Zeus' split head erected one day then replaced by Athena receiving Medusa's head from Perseus the next week. Towards the end of 1956, Hermes installed a chorus of automated mud dolls on the periphery of the store. On all floors, they sang, moved, and played among themselves, letting their bird-like voices resonate through all the floors and all the rooms in the horizontally growing building. It is said that the songs of the singing mud dolls were reflective of Hermes Uy's mood. Yet, for all the sad and happy, bitter and lovesick songs of the dolls, nobody knew much of what Hermes had become. So, it was to the great shock of most on Christmas Day 1956, that the dolls began to sing Christian hymns.

While no one is sure if Hermes really did convert to Christianity a few days before the dolls began singing Christian hymns, it still remains an interesting possibility. Around this time, the newer additions to Athena Drugstore were mostly empty rooms of gold carpet and white paint. And so, people naturally figured that Hermes might have found the calling of the true faith, spending more time in the church than loafing around his drugstore, trying to see if everything was all right. The empty rooms continued to sprout up, and not a word was ever heard of Hermes until the middle of the next year, when they found his body.

Although no exact records exist, the account of the death of Hermes Uy presented here is judged by most to be the most accurate.

The humid air of that 14 April night was, as always, a bother for Hermes Uy, who had just completed the day dressed as a police officer on his break. He took off his cap, put down his truncheon, and wiped his brow. He had just finished the last of the seventy-nine rooms that made up what was once a simple drugstore. Making his way to the green-hued counter in the middle of the store, he switched on the electric fan. The motor hummed and the blades started turning. *It was wise of me to make the little mud dolls sing Christian hymns*, he thought as he twirled the scapular around his neck. He took out thick ledgers from underneath the table and went through the receipts for the day.

As always, he had made a tidy sum of money.

While he was going over the figures for the day in his customary second round, something caught the corner of his eye. Though the movie stars that graced the Athena Drugstore calendar that hung in one corner were all still there, the image of the goddess was not. Hermes put down his pen and moved closer.

It was definitely gone, the paper still intact but blank. The smiling Athena was really gone. Perplexed, Hermes looked around.

All the images of Athena were gone. There was no trace of her on the posters, murals, and calendars that were scattered all over the room. He realized that they were all gone, all missing from the different items in the seventy-nine rooms and three floors of the drugstore. It was then that he saw them. Two-dimensional bodies of plastic, paint, and paper translucent in the fluorescent glow, flanking the latest version of Athena's bronze statue, an Athena in full battle gear.

Though clunky looking, the statue moved so swiftly that Hermes Uy had no time to move before he was slapped by it. The slap was so strong that Hermes was flung to the floor, his head crushed. As the bronze Athena walked away, the multitude of smaller Athenas rushed towards his body, the plastic ones swaying more fluidly than the ones made of paper.

Quickly, they fell upon him, flat bodies worming their way up his legs, then up his torso, to his neck and face.

Athena Drugstore failed to open the next day. People thought that it was another of Hermes Uy's renovations and paid it little attention. Months, then years passed, with most unaware that not only was Hermes Uy gone from this world, but the doors of Athena Drugstore were never to open again, cobwebs and dust collecting where a goddess once roamed.

A Visit to the Exhibition of
the International Committee
on Children's Rights

We were a bit taken aback when we learned that we would be going to the National Conference Centre to see the visiting exhibition of the International Committee on Children's Rights. After all, we had already gone to the Museum of the Filipino Republic earlier in the year, and with the final exams approaching, a school circular about another field trip was totally unexpected. While we were hardly impressed by the circular, with its formulaic exposition extolling the virtues of the exhibition as a means of bringing awareness to the plight of other children and its usual return slip that had to be signed, acknowledged, and cut by our parents, the news it bore brought a lingering sense of excitement and unease in us.

Though we had all heard about the committee, we struggled to recall what we knew about it. Like Save the Children, CARE, and Greenpeace, the International Committee on Children's Rights was one of those organizations that people nominally recognized while having only vague ideas about their actual activities. Some of us recalled reading in the newspapers that the exhibition had just arrived from Jakarta the other night, and after a few days, would be moving on to Cebu and Davao to complete its first Southeast Asian tour. As far as anyone knew, the committee had been touring the world with its exhibition for the past couple of decades. Strange as this may have seemed, it was apparent from the newspapers that the committee was doing well, since aside from being awarded numerous international citations, it also counted on constant donations from a multicultural array of billionaire philanthropist benefactors.

However, this did not mean that the committee was beyond reproach. The more studious of us remembered the existence of a few critical articles, which were immediately found and circulated through our mailing list. Some of these pieces painted the exhibition as a tasteless gimmick that focused too much on emotions but failed to tackle any of the social, economic, and cultural reasons for the violation of children's rights. Others saw it as an attempt to impose the hegemony of a certain moral code among poorer nations. A few even questioned the usefulness of the committee itself, especially since its activities were seemingly limited to its perpetually touring exhibition.

Since we were generally unable to follow the complex arguments in the articles, we were far more disturbed by the presence of unconfirmed and untraceable rumours that suggested a more sinister side to the committee. It was said that the during the mid-1980s, the committee was banned in several countries in Latin America and Eastern Europe after some visitors experienced mass hallucinations which left them hysterically rambling for hours about their essences being sucked by unseen entities. It was also said that, more recently, the committee had been hiring psychics, shamans, and occultists as part of its circle of consultants. There was even talk of the committee as a front for shady evangelicals who used the exhibition as a way to conduct covert baptisms.

There was little to be known about the exhibition itself. Nothing but a few random sentences directly mentioned it, even in the articles critical of the committee. These little bits of information were at best vague, such as that the contents of the exhibition, which ranged from the cheerful to the macabre, changed daily, and that it was, for better or worse, a life-changing experience for any visitor.

These facts and rumours were a constant source of anxiety and curiosity for us in the days leading up to our visit. Though we constantly thought of the infinite possibilities that the exhibition may bring, at different points we also wondered if we could somehow persuade our parents to not allow us to go or if the field trip could possibly be cancelled. Yet we knew that the school had already called our parents not only to assure them of our safety and well-being but also to inform them that our visit was a rare educational opportunity to deepen our understanding of the school's values through a venue unavailable to previous batches.

And so, whatever concerns and worries we may have had remained unanswered until the day that, all present, we boarded a rented tour bus to the National Conference Centre. Though the unease and uncertainty of the previous week lingered, we shared chips, crackers, and dirty jokes. This was, after all, a field trip, an anomaly in the monotony of student life that somehow, despite the rumours, we welcomed as a distraction from our academic responsibilities and club duties.

Because of heavy traffic, it was only after an hour that we arrived at the National Conference Centre at the bayside boundary of Pasay and Manila. The parking lot was full. We were not the only ones to visit the exhibition, as we saw students from different schools move among the throngs of buses. From the variety of uniforms, it appeared that a good percentage of Manila's schools, both public and private, were represented, almost giving the place the atmosphere of a papal visit.

After alighting from the bus, our teachers led us towards one of the centre's many entrances to take our place among the winding queues. Huge banners emblazoned with four skeletal children of different races squatting within a globe—the seal of the International Committee on Children's Rights—were scattered around the centre's façade. Though the sun seemed to burn the back of our heads and the incessant chattering around us was a source of irritation, the line fortunately moved fast, and within a few minutes, we entered the air-conditioned comfort of the centre's lobby.

Our teachers led us to a corner of the white-tiled lobby and asked us to stay put while they got our tickets from the counter at the opposite end. While waiting, we chatted among ourselves. From where we stood, we could see a pair of black curtains embroidered with the committee's seal a few metres away from the back of the counter. As we discussed the possibilities that lay behind those curtains, the more suave of us tried to draw the girls from the other schools into our conversations. Like us, they knew little of the committee and its exhibition and had been equally surprised when they were informed of their field trip.

This mini soirée was broken up after a few minutes by the arrival of our teachers, who handed each of us a nondescript ticket, and a pair of earphones connected to a small device that was to be strapped to our arms. We were then instructed to pass by the red dots scattered throughout the exhibition proper.

As we moved in two lines towards the black curtains, past the other students who were already beginning to strap on their listening devices, and past the registration counter where we surrendered our tickets, we saw and passed by a red dot on the floor. A red light flickered on our listening devices and a voice with a gruff Scottish accent welcomed us to the exhibition of the International Committee on Children's Rights.

While the voice finished explaining that the exhibition was composed of different rooms that the committee constantly adjusted to suit local and regional concerns, we made our way past the curtains. Though we wondered what the voice meant by that, our listening devices fell silent. We found ourselves in a dark, narrow hallway that led to a room with another red dot at the entrance.

Inside, the walls of the room had glass panels displaying various girls and boys of different ages in the nude. At this point the Scottish voice returned by explaining that this room illustrated the physical aspects of children by showing the physiological diversity among them. Propped up by stands, the display of girls and boys seemed to cut across age and race while apparently being ordered in a chronological manner. The voice directed our attention to the leftmost portion of the room, where we saw a collection of newborn babies of different races, all appearing to be covered by a shiny glaze. The voice explained that these were the remains of real children that were preserved using a special type of plasticine. This news left an odd sense of surprise and fascination among us. Until then, we had no inkling of what we were looking at, and we were a bit surprised at how easy it was to look at something that we would have normally thought terrifying and disturbing.

From the newborn babies, the voice then led us through the exhibition's displays on infants, toddlers, and a wide range of various prepubescent and pre-teen children. Though we were bored by the voice's jargon-laced explanations of the physical changes that happened as a child transited from one stage to the other, we found the female portion of the exhibition's display on adolescents riveting.

In retrospect, the girls behind the glass display that day could have barely been called women. However, since it was the first time most of us had actually seen a naked girl, the sight of budding breasts and the first wisps of pubic hair titillated us. We barely listened to the voice's exposition on puberty as we sheepishly looked at the girls. Though the special plasticine gave their bodies an odd sheen, we somehow got the impression that this was a very natural, albeit rare, sight and continued staring until the voice announced that we had to proceed to the next room.

By this time, we were already standing on the right side of the room, near a brightly illuminated doorway with yet another red dot at its entrance. As we passed by the red dot and into the next room, the voice announced that we had entered the Hall of Recreation.

From where we stood, we could see several rows of shelves stretch out into the shadows. On the shelves was an immense variety of toys, games, and sporting goods—some familiar to us while others we found a bit odd and foreign.

The voice explained that the Hall of Recreation was created because of the importance of recreational activities in the physical, mental, social, and cultural development of every child. The hall contained the most extensive collection of children's recreational materials in the world. This collection was also exhaustive given that its contents continuously grew with every new toy, game, or sport invented.

As the voice spoke, we witnessed new items materialize. Were the hall not so brightly illuminated we would have been more frightened than confused. Toy guns, spears, and swords appeared beside die-cast robots, cars, and planes while different dolls suddenly sat beside tennis rackets, baseball bats, and basketballs. Rocking horses, action figures, and slingshots took their place beside chess sets, board games, and video game consoles as cuddly animals, cricket wickets, and masks appeared alongside kitchen sets, putty, and frisbees. More confusing were the headless dolls, misshapen mud globs, and various kinds of rocks that were scattered on different shelves. As a seemingly infinite array of items sprouted on endless rows of shelves, the voice announced that owing to the nature of the hall, our tour would only take us through a tiny portion of the exhibit.

At the voice's instructions, we started to move forward. We were told that the path that had been designed for our tour was special, since instead of the regular shelves, we were to go through the ones where the new items were held before being placed in the exhibit. As we drew closer, we began to see that on the shelves, behind each item, were thin television monitors that flickered on as soon as we saw them.

Since flat-screen televisions would only become commercially available years later, we were amazed by the sharpness and resolution of the images that flashed on the multitude of monitors. On each screen, a picture of the recreational item in front of it was shown, followed by a series of short clips showing the item being used by different children, whose joy and energy seemed to be magnified by the television screens. After a few seconds, the items would all disappear, making way for another batch of items and videos as they became part of the hall's perpetually growing collection.

Though we were still a bit confused, as we moved around, witnessing fishing rods turn into boomerangs and jackstones give way to plastic dinosaurs, the numerous clips of happy children seemed to rub off. Gradually, an uncontrollable and inexplicable kind of happiness took root in each of us so that we were skipping and humming by the time we reached the other side of the Hall of Recreation.

We were so happy that when the voice announced we were to leave the hall and move on to the next part of the exhibition, we realized we weren't really certain if we had heard it speak since its introduction to the area. And so, while we struggled to suppress our mirth, we made our way through the hall's exit and into the next room.

Unlike the first two rooms, the third area did not have a corridor or a red dot at its entrance. Instead, we immediately found ourselves in a white-carpeted room with several mannequins of different races. These mannequins were all dressed differently. There were male and female mannequins in business suits, lab coats, and various uniforms, while a few were dressed in a more informal manner—the males in boxer shorts and undershirts and the females in tattered dusters.

There was a red dot embedded in the carpet a few metres from the closest mannequin—a Caucasian male wearing a doctor's coat with a stethoscope dangling from its ears. Already accustomed to the exhibition's red dots, each of us walked over it in anticipation of an explanation for such a bland display.

Almost on cue, the voice revealed that this room was created to illustrate how access to a good education was crucial towards unlocking the potential of every child. Because of the uniqueness inherent in each child, the room tried to effect a convergence of life stories in the form of the mannequins, which we were then instructed to approach.

One by one the mannequins started to stir and open their expressionless glass eyes. Then the mannequin nearest to us, the one dressed as a Caucasian doctor, started to speak.

Introducing itself as the late Dr James Smith, the mannequin started by saying that as a child growing up in an American suburb, he had wanted to become an astronaut so that he could visit other planets. However, his mother's death due to cancer led him to decide that he wanted to become a doctor, a goal he finally accomplished a decade later. As a doctor, he had felt good helping the sick and infirm, especially those who had went on to live long and prosperous lives.

As the Dr Smith mannequin talked more about his life, a few of us started to feel a bit bored and began to approach the next mannequin—this time a Chinese-looking male in business attire. In an odd Chinese–British accent, the mannequin said that he was the late Stanley Lim, a Malaysian businessman whose parents immigrated to Malaysia before he was born. Since his family had been poor while growing up, he knew that he wanted to become rich so that his children wouldn't experience hardship. As such, he became very serious about his studies and eventually was able to acquire the skills and experiences necessary to become successful in Malaysia's real estate market.

After a few minutes, we decided to move on to the other mannequins, and left Dr Smith and Mr Lim to their monologues. We moved from mannequin to mannequin, setting off such a varied collection of life stories that within a few minutes, the whole room resonated with the monotonous drone of their voices.

It was soon apparent that the room had both successes and failures. Aside from the American doctor and the Malaysian businessman, there was the Pakistani imam whose diligence at the madrasa gave him the authority to speak about Allah's law, the Moroccan women's rights activist who successfully petitioned the king for the establishment of gender parity measures, and the Filipino human rights lawyer who defended the wrongfully accused during the martial law period. In contrast, there were also mannequins of the Brazilian slum dweller who was content to spend his time drinking cachaça all day, the German woman who was content to stay at home while living on welfare benefits, as well as the Kazakh woman who dropped out of school to become a masseuse in a Macanese massage parlour.

Although we found the mannequins' stories a bit too preachy and did not really care for the fact that they continued to speak even after we had left them, we were a bit disconcerted by the way they referred to themselves in past terms, and how they seemed to convey a feeling of repressed anguish despite their blank faces and monotonous tones. In this sense, we were very relieved when the talking of the mannequins began to wane, their eyes began to close, and the voice returned with directions to proceed to the next area of the exhibition.

The white carpet of the previous room was soon replaced by wood-panelled flooring as we stepped past another red dot and into the exhibition's next part. A few dozen strange machines were scattered in an otherwise insignificant area. Every unit consisted of complex modules that were attached to each other by colourful wires and circuits. Perhaps the most discernible part of these machines were the chairs that we could see through the glass panels on the surface of each contraption. As we pondered the purpose of these machines, the voice told us that the area we were in was called the Viewing Room of Abuses.

The voice continued by saying that although most of the world's countries had already ratified the International Convention on the Protection of the Fundamental Rights of the Child, child abuse still constituted one of the world's more acute problems. Despite the continued efforts of groups such as the International Committee on Children's Rights, child abuse had become a rampant if not lucrative business, especially in developing countries. As such, the Viewing Room of Abuses was created to give viewers an idea of a social disease that had to be stamped out.

At this point, the voice drew our attention towards the strange machines. As we had imagined when we first saw the chairs, each one of us was to be seated in what the voice called a 'viewing unit'. As per the voice's instructions, our teachers led us to be seated inside a viewing unit, where we were strapped with a safety harness and told to remain calm. A few minutes after the hatches were closed, the lights began to dim, and within seconds, we found ourselves in different places and scenarios.

Though each one of us knew that we were still somewhere in the National Conference Centre, our senses were telling us that we were alone in a different space and time. Some of us found ourselves as child labourers, stitching sneakers in hot, cramped Chinese factories where we had to work despite aching hands and parched throats. Others felt the heavy burden of cargo being strapped to their backs as they staggered through the world's piers. There were even a few of us who appeared in Cambodian brothels, looking helplessly as overweight, balding tourists loosened their belts to ask for 'boom-boom'.

As some of us felt the horrors of child abuse rooted in poverty, others experienced a more domestic kind of suffering. While a number of us went through being cursed at, slapped, and punched by drunken parents, a handful became a parish priest's 'little sultana'.

Although we were not sure how long we stayed in those infernal viewing units, the unspeakable horrors during those moments were so intense that, by the time we were brought back and the lights were turned on, most of us—even those known to be bullies in class—were reduced to silent sobbing. At that point, none of us wanted to continue. The only thing we wanted to do was to go home. We took off our earphones and began to unstrap our listening devices from our arms.

To our dismay, the gruff Scottish voice was still audible even without the earphones. Without hesitation, it told us that we were to proceed to the next and final area of the exhibition. At this, we turned to our teachers with angry sobs. Although we all wanted nothing to do with the exhibition, our teachers made it clear that we had no choice but to proceed. This was because the exhibition's path was extremely linear such that there was really only one exit. We then agreed that we would all leave our listening devices, that none of us would walk over a red dot, and that we would all walk swiftly through the next room and out of the National Conference Centre.

With our resolutions, we left the Viewing Room of Abuses and entered a dark, humid corridor with no lights save for different patches of faint colours eerily suspended in the air. Contrary to our expectations, there was no red dot to be seen. As we made our way into the room, the voice welcomed us into the Corridor of the Nameless, the final area of the exhibition.

The voice began by saying that individuality was something that people considered important. Although names generally tended to recur in specific cultural milieus, having a name is crucial in the development of one's individuality. As such, one of the most fundamental rights of every child is to be named and to know their name.

Unfortunately, some children die before being named or getting to know their name. In this context, the International Committee on Children's Rights had decided to pay homage to the memory of the nameless by creating an area for them to collectively gather and be remembered.

While the voice was still speaking, we tried to make our way through the corridor. However, upon reaching the area of the room that had orange particles floating around, we were seized by a happiness that was even more intense than the one we had felt earlier. As we forgot about our problems and began to immerse ourselves in laughter, the voice said that we were standing in the area where all the nameless children who died happy were gathered.

Our laughter continued for a few more minutes until it slowed down and finally disappeared along with the orange particles. Still grinning, we walked towards the area with blue particles, where we were overwhelmed by a tremendous melancholia and depression. At this, the voice announced that we had reached the area where the nameless children who died sad were gathered.

A pattern then became clear. After a few minutes, we would be able to regain our composure albeit still feeling the effects of the coloured particles, which by then would have vanished. Then, we would move into another area with a different set of floating particles that triggered an emotion that corresponded to that of the nameless babies at their time of death. This emotion would render us helpless until the pattern began all over again.

This pattern held true for most of the subsequent areas. For example, in the area with the red particles, which supposedly contained the children who had died angry, we became prone to an outburst of anger that had us shouting and nearly coming to blows with one another. In much the same way, the area where the nameless children who died selfish and envious—where the green particles floated, had us obsessively touching our pockets while keeping a close eye on one another.

However, the pattern would prove to be relative. As we approached the last area before the exit—where white particles formed a thick haze above the floor, we felt a distilled kind of nothingness, a deep kind of numbness that left us devoid of any emotions. The voice then said that the area housed the stillborn and aborted babies.

As we passed through the exit, the voice thanked us for visiting the Exhibition of the International Committee on Children's Rights. Back on the bus, we were all silent. When we got home, we all told our parents that the trip was all right and did not add any other details. During the next few days of school, no one talked about the field trip in public, and although we had originally thought that our teachers would ask for a reflection paper or conduct a quiz about our visit, no such requirement ever came up.

The months, then years passed, and we went on with our lives, going through school, marrying, and fathering children, barely remembering the Visiting Exhibition of the International Committee on Childrens' Rights except during sudden, seemingly tangential instances or in the nightmares that took us back to hear the voice's gruff monotone in our sleep.

An Epistle and Testimony
from 13 June 1604

During the renovation of the Madrid city archives in August 1999, a letter, together with an attached manuscript, was found. Together, these caused a stir in both historical and theological circles. Though initially branded as a hoax, testing indicated that both the letter and the manuscript were contemporaneous to their stated date, with the name of Padre Tomas Rodriguez also being present in the registry of Dominican missionaries sent to the Philippines during the early seventeenth century. However, some historians have pointed out that some significant historical events have been left unmentioned. Moreover, attempts at content analysis have not been able to conclusively address speculation that the manuscript is nothing more than seventeenth century religious propaganda. As such, the letter and the manuscript, their full text translated from the Spanish and reproduced below, are still subject to much debate.

Pax Christi. Glory to the Lord.

Last year, I wrote to you of the circumstances surrounding my voyage from Nueva España to this city of Manila, as well as a brief description of the city from one so unacquainted with the Indies. Over the past year, Padre Gonzales and I have busied ourselves with seeing to the needs of the Order's hospital near the Parian, the Chinese quarter outside the city walls. We have learned enough of the language to engage the Sangleys in simple conversation and hope to begin instructing them in matters of the faith within the following year.

Doubtless word has already reached Madrid of the manner and circumstances of the Sangleys, as well as the Chinese revolt that happened on the feast of San Francisco the previous year. I have no doubt that it also has been known that thousands of Sangleys have been put to death for conspiring in this affair, which saw the martyrdom of Padre Bernardo de Santa Catalina, among many others of the faith, at the hands of the Sangley infidels, who, it is said, lost heart at the miraculous apparitions of our crucified Lord and San Fransisco during the melee. For this reason, and therefore to save you from any inconvenience, I shall say little of the circumstances surrounding all this, except that which directly concerns my person as well as what I am about to relate to you.

From the time I have spent in the Parian, I have no doubt that what our countrymen have been saying—not only are the Sangleys a shrewd and cunning race, always greedy for money but also keeping hold of the necessities of the city, so much so that the natives are regulated to their inherent idleness—has some truth. However, I too have seen numerous exceptions to this, having encountered Sangleys that have been exemplary in their piety and faithfulness to both our Lord and our faith throughout the past year, as well as Sangleys that, priest that I am, have shown me wonders that I struggle to comprehend. Such a wonder was exemplified by a certain Tu Tzu-Ch'un, also known as Lazaro de Chino, who seemed to carry the wounds of our Lord Himself and whose perplexing and terrifying fate I can only relay through this manuscript that I am attaching to this letter. I pray that you may be able to furnish this manuscript, entitled *The Wondrous Case of Lazaro de Chino during the Revolt of the Infidel Sangleys in Manila*, in its entirety to the Brothers de Joya, whose success in the publishing of true accounts from Nueva España and beyond has been unmatched.

The Wondrous Case of Lazaro de Chino during the Revolt of the Infidel Sangleys in Manila

I first learned of Lazaro through the traitor Juan Bautista de Vera, a Christian Sangley otherwise known as Eng Kang who, before being executed for his treason, held office as governor of the Chinese, both Christian and pagan. A few months after taking over the administration of the hospital, following the demise of the beloved Padre Domingo, whose pious life our Lord will certainly notice and reward in paradise, both Padre Gonzales and myself were extended invitations to an informal gathering on the eve of the feast of Santa Catalina de Siena by the Chinese Christians.

During the course of the festivities, the coward de Vera, in whose house the gathering was being held, approached me. His breath reeking of wine, he asked if he could speak to me in private. I could only nod and stare at his rotting teeth. de Vera led me to the corner of the room, then asked that no other party be privy to the contents of our conversation—something that although not unreasonable, I am obliged to break given the present circumstances, for without doing so, I will not be able to relate the events surrounding Lazaro de Chino. De Vera then informed me that the previous Friday, one of the Christian Sangleys in Binondo had been afflicted by a strange malady.

According to de Vera, at around 3.00 p.m., Lazaro's wife, a native who was with child, was roused from her nap by a scream. She found Lazaro lying on the floor in a feverish delirium, his hands clasped in prayer around the holy rosary. Later, upon being roused from his fit by his wife and some of his neighbours—all Christian Sangleys—Lazaro claimed that a winged seraph had visited him while he was praying, and in a voice that was not of this world, asked him to share in the wounds and suffering of our Saviour. Without giving him a chance to answer, the seraph then extended its arms, and a dazzling and painful light enveloped Lazaro's hands. The people present were inclined to believe this to be symptomatic of his delirium; however, when they saw that on Lazaro's hands were wounds out of which flowed blood with the fragrance of incense, they became excited and proceeded to call de Vera so that they could conduct themselves in an orderly manner. de Vera issued orders that no news of this event was to be heard on the streets, under the punishment of death. I have no doubt that the reason for this was that de Vera did not know what to do with such a perplexing and wondrous event. Not only this but I also suspect that this was precisely the reason why he had sought to obtain my counsel on the matter.

As I was intrigued by his story, I asked him the circumstances of this Lazaro de Chino. Why would a Sangley, a recent convert who would normally apostatize at the first sight of silver, be so blessed to bear the marks of our Saviour?

de Vera replied that Lazaro had been born in Ch'angan to a landed family. In his youth he had left his families' lands in a state of neglect, and like the young San Agustin, he had greatly indulged in pleasures of the flesh. Likewise, he squandered his inheritance and soon found himself in debt and as a fugitive from his numerous creditors. He escaped on a junk laden with goods and found himself in Manila a few months later.

At this point, it should be known that despite the restrictions limiting the amount of Sangleys in the Parian, a Sangley wanting to stay in the colony could do so with ease, given the huge number of Sangleys already in the city. Thus, it is of no surprise that Lazaro was able to wander around, still without anything to his name. According to de Vera, Lazaro spent most of his nights near the vicinity of the Order's hospital, where under the guidance of Padre Domingo, he was baptized. He adopted his Christian name and eventually took one of the natives as his bride, settling down in Binondo while learning the trade of stone carving.

After listening to the story of Lazaro de Chino's conversion, I became even more intrigued. I asked de Vera what kind of Christian the man was. He replied that Lazaro was deeply religious and, through the guidance of Padre Domingo, was wont to receive the Holy Eucharist daily and diligently fast on Fridays. Lazaro also became an avid reader of the Book of Hours, of which a translation had been made by Padre Domingo. de Vera also added that Lazaro had also done numerous charitable actions, to which his neighbours would certainly attest. This being said, I told de Vera that if it were possible, I would be pleased to meet such an individual. de Vera stood silent for a moment, apparently trying to assess the consequences of such a meeting. Then, he said yes. He would be happy to introduce me to Lazaro de Chino, who without doubt would be pleased to meet the successor of Padre Domingo.

It was five days later, on 5 May, a terribly rainy Monday nonetheless, that de Vera led me through the narrow Binondo streets to meet Lazaro, whose house stood near the vicinity of the church. The pouring rain turned the streets ashen, and by the time we arrived at Lazaro's house, both de Vera and myself were soaked.

As doubtless, word of the smallness of the typical Sangley house has already been made known in Madrid, I can merely say that the house of Lazaro was characteristic of his race. Lazaro's wife, a homely native in the first months of her pregnancy, ushered us in and proceeded to call her husband.

How shall I describe the man who had been the cause of my great excitement over the past few days? I must confess that in my excitement, I had imagined Lazaro to be a Chinese San Fransisco, chosen by our Lord to share in His pain and suffering and in His simplicity and wretchedness while having both greatness and strength as well. In reality, Lazaro's features did not stand out in any way. He was dressed in the typicality of his race, and save for the bandages wrapped around his hands, there was nothing to distinguish him from his Christian countrymen.

de Vera greeted Lazaro, then introduced me as Padre Domingo's successor. Whereupon Lazaro bowed to de Vera and then to me. He greeted us in the Chinese tongue then bade us to sit down in broken Castilian.

de Vera told him of the purpose of our visit. 'Padre Rodriguez is interested in what happened to you two Fridays ago. Perhaps you can explain it to him yourself,' he addressed Lazaro with that uncouth mouth of his. At these words Lazaro nodded and looked at me, then asked if I had, indeed, succeeded Padre Domingo. I nodded.

'Padre Domingo was a good man,' he added in his broken Castilian while he shook his head vigorously. I did not understand why he did not want to talk about the events that de Vera had told me so much about. Was he afraid of something? Only now do I realize that rarely in the Sangley mind can de Vera's directness be found, and during that time I could only nod and agree with him.

'Padre, when I first arrived in this city I had nothing but my clothes. I spent most of my days and nights begging for food near the Christian hospital.' With that he related how he met Padre Domingo. 'I used to see him walking to and from the hospital every day. I did not think he noticed me, but one day, he stopped and asked me why I was there every day. "Do you not have a family to support?" he had asked. I said I had none. He then asked for the reasons for my being there. I told him that I had spent all my money on rich food, wine, and women and that I had to leave because the people to whom I owed money had threatened to kill me. To this Padre Domingo asked if I thought money was really my problem. I replied that I had given much thought to this topic, and that I had concluded that I had lived a life that ill-fitted my family's fortunes. If I had the fortunes of a high-level mandarin, I would be able to live a life of comfort for the rest of my days.'

Having heard this, Padre Domingo gave Lazaro a few pieces of silver, telling him to live the life he wanted for that day. If the money would run out tomorrow, he would gladly replenish it the following day. Though I had always known that Padre Domingo was a good man, this was the first account I heard about him giving out money. I found this strange, especially considering his peasant origins. Doubtless, Padre Domingo had a source of income other than the Order's treasury, for all the pieces of silver in our hands have been accounted for. However, uncovering this source of income would be most difficult because of the plentiful possibilities for earning money in the city, and for this reason, I shall make no further mention of this.

Let me now continue the account related to me by Lazaro. After he had been given the silver, Lazaro said that he tried to spend the money wisely, breaking his morning fast with the simplest and cheapest gruel to be found in the city. But, in the course of the day, he began buying food and drink that, although inferior to the kind he had enjoyed while still in China, was expensive. And so, by the time the sun had set, Lazaro once again found himself no better off than he had been when he first arrived in the city.

True to his word, Padre Domingo passed by the next morning. He asked Lazaro if he had lived satisfactorily the previous day and if he thought the money he had given him was sufficient. To this Lazaro said that although he wholeheartedly gave his thanks to Padre Domingo for his charitable deed, even before the end of the previous day not a single silver piece was remaining. According to Lazaro, Padre Domingo smiled upon hearing these words, and then asked if he indeed needed more money to live a life of comfort. Lazaro then said that he could only nod his head at these words, as he was still too embarrassed to speak. Padre Domingo then tripled the silver he had given Lazaro the previous day and after giving him the same instructions as before, left.

After Padre Domingo had left, Lazaro said that he made a promise to himself. He would manage his money with diligence, so much so that he would be able to return to China, pay off all his debts, and live a life greater than the legendary mandarins. Yet, once again, he did not succeed in this, with all his money being spent on pleasures of the flesh before the sun had set.

By the time he had realized this, Lazaro said that he became mortified and could only wait until morning for Padre Domingo to arrive. Padre Domingo arrived at his usual hour, and upon seeing Lazaro, walked towards him.

By this time Lazaro had become excited. His face became more animated and he seemed to forget my presence as he talked quickly in a mix of the Chinese and Castilian tongues, almost as he was looking at something beyond myself. Since my own comprehension of his speech was inadequate, I had difficulty understanding his exact words. However, it would appear that after learning of Lazaro's inability to manage the money given to him, Padre Domingo had pressed even more money on him. He apparently gave Lazaro the same instructions as before, but this time saying that if he was not able to make do with that amount, which was equal to forty times a workman's daily wage then there would not be much use in giving him any more money. According to Lazaro, the words of Padre Domingo had moved him to tears, as he realized that the problem was not that he lacked money but that he was always using it wrongly. He told Padre Domingo that he had been drawn to luxury and had been ambitious and greedy. Being devoid of luxury, ambition, and greed had not been enough, since he was wont towards these things even when he had no money. As he was saying this, Padre Domingo kept silent and only smiled. Lazaro then promised to use the money Padre Domingo gave him not for his comfort but to put most of it in the service of orphans and widows. At these words, Padre Domingo asked him if he was really willing to leave his love of luxury behind. Lazaro said yes. At that, Padre Domingo taught him about our Saviour Jesus Christ and the faith.

With that, Lazaro finished his account of his conversion. He had thrown himself into his new faith with vigour, trying to become the best Christian he could possibly be to the extent of his faculties. I could still hear the rain falling outside. However unorthodox Padre Domingo may have been, that he had brought about a pious convert from the Sangleys was a cause for joy. I thought about how Saul had been converted by our Lord from one who hated the Christians to San Pablo—who sacrificed his life for the Church. Truly there is no one who is deaf to His word!

'Padre, even after I was baptized, I did not consider myself a Christian yet,' Lazaro said after a few moments of silence. I looked up. Lazaro's look was focused, and all his words once again became slow and deliberate. 'Because for me, a Christian is one who is willing to share in our Lord's words and suffering. At that stage in my life I was not ready to share in Christ's suffering even if I held His words to my heart and tried to love others as He had loved us all. I could not comprehend how much He suffered.' I found the Sangley's words touching, and I began to reflect if I myself would be willing to share in the agony that our Lord went through. I imagined the stinging sharpness of the crown of thorns, the heavy weight of the cross, the hot pain of each nail driven through both skin and bone, and the final pain of the spear thrust in addition to all the humiliation He suffered. Until now, I do not know if I would be willing to go through everything our Lord sacrificed for us.

Lazaro then said that he had taken the Holy Eucharist a few weeks after his conversion. At the first touch of the Holy Eucharist, Lazaro had felt that every bit of Tu Tzu-Ch'un was replaced by a presence of joy and sorrow. A few months later, he married a Christian native and settled in their present house while trying to learn the skills of a stone carver in order to provide for his household.

By this time, I began to feel weary and looked at de Vera, who shot me a look that conveyed his understanding. We excused ourselves and, after expressing our gratitude to Lazaro and his wife, left.

It was still raining that night. Not being able to sleep, I pondered on the events of the past few days. I had not been given the answers I wanted and had yet to even see the wounds of Lazaro de Chino. I thought that while his digression was typical of his race, his direct avoidance of the topic was unreasonable even for a Sangley. I could not gauge the man's thoughts. Was it because de Vera was present?

I was even tempted to think that everything de Vera and Lazaro told me was false. Surely, they had no reason to do so. The ancient Greeks would never have fared well in this city. However, I resolved to put my faith in the Lord and find out the circumstances of the mystery surrounding this Lazaro de Chino for the greater glory of the faith.

Accompanied by a Sangley coolie sent by de Vera, I visited Lazaro again a few weeks later, on 27 May. de Vera was unable to accompany me because of the demands of his position—three mandarins, together with their entourage of servants, secretaries, and the like, had arrived 23 May and presented themselves to Governor Acuna as emissaries of the emperor. As governor of the Sangleys, de Vera was supposed to see to their needs and entertainment. I have no doubt that it was during those days that the Sangley uprising was planned, as I would learn later that de Vera had begun to incite the Sangleys and collected numerous armaments shortly after the said visit of these three mandarins was completed.

The sky was downcast when I arrived at the house of Lazaro, whose wife immediately saw to my needs despite my protests for her to do otherwise, lest she upset her condition. I told the coolie to come back after an hour had passed. Lazaro came out after a few minutes. As he bowed to me in the Sangley manner, I noticed that his hands were unbound.

At that time, I could only think that truly only God could bestow such a gift that can never be comprehended by man! On each of his hands were wounds that seemed as if nails were driven through them. Each wound was bright red. The heads of the nails could be seen on the palms of his hands.

Since scabs had yet to form, I could see light through each of Lazaro's hands, which indeed, smelled of incense.

Lazaro must have noticed the attention I was paying to his wounds for he asked his wife to bind them. While his wife bound each hand tightly, Lazaro spoke. 'Now that you've seen them, Padre, tell me—what do you think?' This outburst was not only uncharacteristic of the Lazaro de Chino who had told me of his conversion to the faith only a few days before, but it was also uncharacteristic of his race. 'I think the wounds are proof that you are in our Lord's favour,' was what I could only mumble at that point.

Lazaro nodded his head. 'I cannot explain it, Padre, but I've always felt that no matter what happens to me, no matter what I do, I can never be truly a Christian.' He held his hands to his face. I noticed that the bandages were beginning to be stained. 'You do understand, right, Padre? No one understands.' I must admit that I did not understand what he was saying, and although I felt that I should say something to put the Sangley at ease, I could not. 'Why so, my son?'

'Because I still cannot say that I am a true Christian. I am neither like you nor Padre Domingo. Even if I love our Lord very much, I do not know if I am worthy to share in his suffering.'

'To share in our Lord's suffering is a calling that all of us hear but can never fully answer,' I replied, although I was unsure if this was true. Had not our martyrs put our Lord above their lives? Did this mean that my journey here is, in truth, of no consequence? I realized that I was mistaken in my words, especially since we of the faith, despite not being martyrs, have given our lives in the service of our Lord for whose sake we would readily lay down our lives. 'Although we can all strive to act in our own little ways to make certain that our Lord's suffering was not in vain,' I added in order to lessen the impact of my error.

Lazaro stared at me with his slit eyes for a few moments. I found it hard to read his thoughts, as his face was without any emotion. Then, in a voice that was barely audible, he whispered that he had witnessed and felt our Lord's pain on the day the seraph came to him.

'Padre, I should have told you earlier, but I was scared,' he said. 'The moment a lot of people find out what happened would mean the end of my life as I have lived it.' I looked at the Sangley's face. Indeed, the presence of fear and desperation were palpable.

'My son, I promise that you will be able to live as you have lived. Did not our Lord heal the blind and cure the sick because of their faithfulness? Surely, He will not forget you!' At these words, the Sangley took in a deep breath and began to narrate the events surrounding the miraculous gift of his wounds.

As de Vera had already told me, Lazaro was praying the rosary that Friday afternoon, after he had arrived from the stone quarry that morning. At exactly 3.00 p.m., the hour of our Lord's death, after he had just finished the first sorrowful mystery, he was blinded by a bright radiance that was unlike any he had seen. A beautiful, winged creature appeared and addressed him without words. Through its wordless language, the seraph told him that his conversion and perseverance had deemed him, through a special provision by God, to become transformed in the likeness of the Lord. The seraph then spread its wings and two darts of light the colour of blood struck Lazaro in both hands. Lazaro said that at that moment he felt an intense pain, so much so that he could do nothing but cry out and lose consciousness. I asked him when he was able to regain control of the faculties of his mind and body.

'I am not certain, Padre,' Lazaro replied. 'I remember awakening in a garden. It was night-time, and aside from myself, there were only four people there. One of them was kneeling in prayer. The other three were asleep. Moving closer, I was shocked to see that it was none other than our Lord Himself that was the one praying!'

I trembled at the Sangley's revelation. Was this possibly true? At that time, I understood that although I wanted to believe, part of me still was in disbelief. I thought that this was probably what Santo Tomas felt when he faced our resurrected Lord for the first time. 'How are you sure that it was our Lord you saw?' I tried to control the tone of my voice.

'He looked like in the painting of our church,' said Lazaro. 'Only his features were livelier. His blue eyes were overflowing with tears as he clenched his fists in prayer. He did not seem to notice anything—not even the snoring of the disciples. It was like everything was frozen, Padre. I felt our Lord's sadness as he prayed. His sadness made me cry.'

Lazaro then described how he suddenly saw our Lord in the possession of the Romans. 'I did not see them arrive, Padre. It was as if our Lord and His weeping faded, and He suddenly was being held by two Roman soldiers. Behind them was a crowd of people whose faces I could not really see. The apostles were already awake, standing helplessly at the side of the garden. One of the three had a drawn dagger in his hand. I could see blood dripping down the blade. The apostle with the drawn dagger was looking at our Lord. I then saw that one of the Roman soldiers' ears was bleeding. The blood poured down the soldier's chin in a long steam and, after a few moments, disappeared. Then there appeared to be no wound on the soldier.'

'Did you see our Lord touch the soldier's ear in the manner of what is written in the scriptures?' I asked. Lazaro said no. 'No one was moving, Padre. Everyone just stood in their places as if they were statues. But I could see that they were real. Their eyes were all fixated on our Lord, whose face looked like it contained all the sorrow in the world.'

Lazaro then continued, saying that after a few moments all the people, including our Lord Himself, faded with the garden. Lazaro then saw Him in front of a tribunal of three people with white, overflowing beards. 'I did not feel at ease with the looks on their faces, Padre,' he said. 'I could see that their distinguished dress and cultivated manners were deceiving. Their faces were full of scorn and spite. One of them even had a finger pointed at our Lord, who held His gaze to the ground. After a few minutes, the tribunal disappeared, and our Lord was left in this same manner, but this time in front of a portly man, who was washing his hands in a brass basin held by two servants. The portly man appeared to be addressing someone other than our Lord, who remained motionless. I turned around and saw a crowd of people assembled below the balcony. I could not see their faces, but I felt their burning hatred. It was too much to bear, Padre. I could only think about how these people who jeered and mocked our Lord might have once loved Him. The Lord may have felt the same way because it seemed as if we were sharing in His sorrow. At that point, I was already trembling. I longed for my wife's touch and wept.'

When Lazaro spoke these words, I must confess that I could not help but think that the loneliness which is inherent in our lives in the Indies, without even the smallest of pleasures so easily found in Spain, is of no comparison to the one our Lord suffered in his supreme sacrifice. I found it astonishing how our Lord went past any apprehensions, loneliness, and fears that He may have had. The will of God is truly supreme! On account of this realization, I felt rejuvenated.

At that point, Lazaro must have noticed that my thoughts were elsewhere, for he ceased to speak and began to watch the shadow of the candle's flame flicker. I told him to continue with his tale.

With his slit eyes narrowing, Lazaro resumed his narration, this time in a more subdued voice. He said that although the crowd, the plump man, and even our Lord eventually faded and disappeared, he felt our Lord's loneliness and sorrow only intensify, so much so that he was reduced to weeping as the next figures were beginning to materialize.

'Next, I saw our Lord tied to a pillar. There was a soldier holding a whip behind Him. I did not see the soldier whip Him, but I knew that they were doing so. With every lash I felt my skin tear off. I felt like I was going to die. While I fell on my belly and prayed for the pain to stop, the Lord stood still. I could see His blue eyes overflowing with pain.'

'Did the pain stop, my son?'

'No, Padre. After a while I thought it had stopped. Our Lord was still standing at the pillar. But the soldiers began to fade and disappear. They reappeared closer to where our Lord was standing. One of them was standing in front of Him. Suddenly, I felt a sharp pain on my head. A crown of thorns appeared on our Lord's head. It was so painful that I could do nothing else but weep. Blood dripped down our Lord's face. Through my tears, I saw my sight turning red as blood dripped into my eyes. The faces of the soldiers were full of amusement and mockery. Yet, at the time, I could barely feel the humiliation because of the pain,' Lazaro paused. He seemed to be staring at something heavenly as his gaze remained transfixed on the candle flame for a few moments.

'Then, what happened?' I had to ask, since I felt I had the obligation to further the interests of both our faith and the truth, whose authorities would be severely compromised if the Sangley's account was not heard and verified.

'After our Lord and the soldiers disappeared, I found myself up a barren hill. A lot of people were gathered along the path. Again, I could not see their faces, but I knew that they were excited. It seemed to be a festive occasion. I suddenly felt an immense burden on my shoulders and had to sit down on the ground. I then saw our Lord carrying His cross. I could see the dried blood on His clothes and the weariness on His face. As much as I wanted to help Him, I couldn't because of the weight that was also bearing down on my shoulders. Our Lord was flanked by rows of soldiers on both sides. Although I could see no one move, I knew that our Lord was dragging the cross with His battered body up the hill, since my knees creaked and my back ached as I stood in my place. I felt our Lord stumble thrice, each time feeling the heavy weight of the cross fall on His back and tasting the dry soil of the path. On one occasion, I felt the burden lighten and saw a man carry the Lord's cross. But after a few minutes, the man disappeared too, and the burden was the Lord's again. I don't know how to describe what I felt during that time, Padre. It seemed that I felt all sorts of emotions. I did not know whether I was grieving, angry, lonely, or fulfilled. Perhaps a little of all.'

At that point, Lazaro was speaking rapidly, his mastery of the Castilian tongue faltering as he bombarded me with phrases that, although I admittedly had difficulty understanding, I nonetheless took pains in reconstructing. It seemed that after seeing our Lord on His way up the Place of the Skull, and after having seemingly served as a witness to the multitude of feelings and emotions our Lord must have felt on His way of the cross, Lazaro found himself on top of the hill. The corpses and bones of the previously crucified lay around him. Lazaro then saw the soldiers lay our Lord down on His cross. Likewise, he also said that there were two other prisoners being laid down on their crosses. Noting that he did not see the actual blows, with this scene, like the others before it, being comprised of the most vivid pictures, Lazaro said that he felt the nails being hammered through our Lord's palms, puncturing both flesh and bone. Lazaro then said that during that moment, there was nothing left for him to do but writhe on the ground in pain. He then felt the Lord's feet being nailed to the cross, more forcefully than His hands. Lazaro said that he was in so much pain that he only fleetingly saw that the soldiers as well as our Lord Himself, who was just nailed to the cross. The pain did not stop for a moment as Lazaro saw our Lord as well as his two companions already crucified, with the soldiers standing beneath their crosses.

Lazaro took a moment's pause, then said that at that point, he had seen a look that was both serene and pained on our Lord's face. Since I could not adequately envision such a thing, I asked him to expound on his statement. However, this was of no use, as he said that he would be unable to further elaborate on what he saw on the Lord's face, as there was nothing really comparable to what he had seen. Lazaro then said that he felt a spear pierce the Lord's ribs into His heart. But for the Sangley at that point it seemed that it mattered little, since it was just another wound on an exhausted and dying body. Lazaro then said that he felt his body go limp, and before he lost consciousness, he heard the only words spoken in the whole duration of his vision—'*Eloi, Eloi, lem, sabachthani?*'

With that, Lazaro ended his tale. He said that he had woken up with his wife, neighbours, and even the governor of the Sangleys at his side. Strangely, it was only his hands that continued to bleed and hurt, with barely a trace of our Saviour's suffering on the other parts of his person. Since it was getting late, Lazaro's wife served a supper of a little rice and fish, and I, together with de Vera's servant, who had been waiting outside Lazaro's house for the past few hours, partook of the simple meal. After having eaten, I bid goodbye to both Lazaro and his wife, and before I left the house, she whispered to me to come the following Friday at 3.00 p.m. to witness what her husband had been talking about earlier.

I must admit that I was very excited upon leaving Lazaro's house. The possibility of a Sangley who would not be able to go back to China without severe consequences, on account of an evil life and numerous debts, converting and claiming to have experienced things that only the blessed have showed me that our Lord's grace is without any pretext. As such, the lives of the countless missionaries sent to the different colonies have surely not been in vain. I thought of the possibility of not only the Sangleys becoming true believers but also of China becoming a nation of believers. Truly, such a move would be possible only if an understanding of the Chinese mind would be reached. But how can such a thing be achieved?

Such were the thoughts that kept me preoccupied during the next few days, during which I also decided that any report about the circumstances of Lazaro de Chino had to be substantiated with more evidence. Although I was undoubtedly amazed by Lazaro's wounds as well as his tale, further proof would be needed to erase any doubt that I may have had to vouch for the Sangley's story. It is on this account that I decided to put to mind the words of Lazaro's wife and visit on Friday, 6 June, at 3.00 p.m., eleven days after my last visit.

By that time I had twice visited Lazaro and, as such, was able to visit the place unaccompanied. A slight drizzle notwithstanding, I was able to reach the house without inconvenience. Lazaro's wife again let me in and despite the burden of her pregnancy, led me past the table where Lazaro and I had conversed the previous times, and into their bedroom.

Lazaro was lying down on a cot. His face was deathly pale and a moustache and beard, traits uncharacteristic of his race, had grown over the past few days. He appeared to be asleep, so I quietly sat down as Lazaro's wife left to attend to her own concerns.

At exactly 3.00 p.m., a series of events happened that I would be ashamed to even write about were I not there to witness it. At that stated time, Lazaro suddenly opened his eyes and stared at something beyond the confines of the room. To my amazement, his eyes had turned deep blue in colour, and his face was contorted in a sorrow unlike any I have ever seen. For one moment I had the feeling that he was about to shed tears, but none were shed.

For a few moments Lazaro was of this manner. However, his face abruptly changed, with his eyes becoming downcast despite him being laid down on his cot, and so did the way his features were contorted. While the sadness and pain on Lazaro's face were still visible, it seemed as if he were concentrating on the judgment passed by an invisible tribunal that heard the accusations against our Lord. Suddenly, he began thrashing around on his cot. Streaks of dark red blood began to appear all over his garments as he grimaced in pain. It was a truly terrifying and amazing thing to behold, as I thought I heard a crack of a whip with every streak of blood smeared on his clothes. A spasm of fear suddenly came over me as Lazaro's body slowly rose over his cot. I almost succumbed to the temptation of cowardice but remained steadfast at the thought of my vocation to our faith and our Lord.

There were no new streaks of blood seen on his person as he lay suspended in the air by the power of forces beyond comprehension. After a few seconds, rows of blood appeared on his forehead, dripping down to his ears and onto his cot. His face remained in a state of pain that I know not how to illustrate in words. Next, it seemed as if a heavy weight was entrusted to Lazaro, as his body appeared to droop. This made his suspension in the air appear to be uneven in nature. His feet and legs also appeared to be shaking as they dragged through the air. Lazaro then stretched both his arms in such a way that it appeared as if he were going to embrace something. However, his arms did not embrace anything as the wounds on his hands, which had been dry until this point, suddenly opened and bled.

The blood on Lazaro's hands flowed down his palms, dripping onto his cot, spreading the smell of incense throughout the room. In a few moments, Lazaro's feet, which previously had not borne marks of any kind, also bled, with a wound on the right foot appearing before the left. Still suspended in the air, he suddenly turned upright, with the blood from his hands and feet pouring harder on his cot. Lazaro remained in this manner for a few moments. I must confess that never in my life had I seen so much blood and, as such, felt so terrified that had I not been petrified, I would have bolted out the house during that time. As I tried to listen to the sound of my breathing in an attempt to calm myself down, Lazaro started bleeding even more, with a wound appearing over the area around his heart. Watching him I felt as if all his vital liquids would be drained. Then, in a barely audible voice, he appeared to mutter a few words and started to descend. He was so pale that I thought I had seen the most vivid image of death.

Now lying prostrate on his cot, Lazaro appeared to have been drained of any life he may have had. In minutes, his wife went into the room and, asking if I was all right, said that she would see to Lazaro's needs and told me that it would be to the best of my interest if I were to go home, since he would still take a few hours to awaken.

Such was what I experienced the next two times I was able to visit the house of the Sangley—on 25 July as well as 22 August. However, on Friday, 5 September, I insisted to

Lazaro's wife that I should stay after he had finished with his visions. Despite her admonitions for me to do otherwise, I remained seated and waited for Lazaro to be roused. Looking at the Sangley's face, I realized that in the course of his visions, more than his eyes had changed. His whole face had changed as well in such a way that he began to resemble an Oriental version of our Lord Himself. What I mean by this is that the Sangley's other facial features—his nose, his mouth, and even his cheeks, had begun to appear less Chinese, taking on the characteristics of not just any white man, but of our Lord. Lazaro's wife took off his bloodied garments. Surprisingly, the wounds on his feet as well as his heart had begun to fade. Accordingly, his face also started to revert to that which is characteristic of his race, with his mouth, nose, and even eyes beginning to constrict. By the time his eyes appeared to be slits once more, only the wounds on both hands remained. Since the wounds on his hands appeared to be dry by this time, it would have been unbelievable for me to think that what had taken place a few hours earlier was true had I not been there to witness it. Lazaro then appeared as before, even regaining his original colour. Although Lazaro stirred from his rest after a few minutes, I must confess that I was unable to converse with him on that occasion, as he was disoriented and, as such, barely coherent when I tried to talk to him.

The next few days proved to be worrisome. In the weeks that had passed since the departure of the three mandarins, talk had begun to circulate that a Chinese fleet would be arriving in Manila within the next year. Since our galleons were only few in number, owing to the departure of the Jesus Maria and Espiritu Santo for Nueva España, as well as the deployment of the Santiago for Japan, there was already much talk among the Sangleys as well as the clergy of the possibility of a Chinese invasion, so much so that the topic became that source of most of the conversations in the city. Accordingly, Governor Acuna took measures to prevent such a tragedy from happening, strengthening the fortification of the city, as well as enlisting the help of the Indians from the province of Pampanga, in addition to the Japanese, who are hostile to the Chinese, to defend the city from any attack launched by the Sangleys. It was only later that it came to my knowledge that during this time, the traitor de Vera had begun, with the aid of his countrymen, the construction of a fort in Tondo. How such a thing happened without our knowledge, I do not know—perhaps serving as a testament to the cunning of the Sangleys.

On Friday, 26 September, I once again paid a visit to Lazaro de Chino. However, because of the heavy pouring of rain, as well as a meeting with the archbishop on the situation of the Sangleys living in the vicinity of the Order's hospital, in addition to the still-unverified reports of people seeing a Black woman who had declared that morning that a great fire and much bloodshed would coincide with the feast of San Francisco, it was already evening when I arrived at Lazaro's house.

After being let in by Lazaro's wife, who appeared nervous and worried, I found Lazaro sitting down on the floor. His eyes were red, and he appeared as pale as he had been during the times that his vision had just concluded. After acknowledging my presence with a nod, he spoke in a barely audible voice, both in Castilian and in his own native tongue. What Lazaro told me was so terrible that I was unable to speak for the next few days. In fact, my hand still trembles as I write this, which due to Lazaro's occasional incoherence and his predilection for speaking in both languages, I am unable to relate word for word.

According to Lazaro, at the appointed time a bright light once again appeared. However, it was not a winged seraph that appeared before him but a distinguished-looking old, Taoist priest bearing three glowing pellets, the light from which hit both his hands, as well as his heart. Lazaro lost consciousness, and when he awakened, found himself in a barren cistern, which was filled with murky water. From where he stood, Lazaro said that he could make out the shapes of a few people gathered together, as well as the faint sound of wailing, which grew louder as he approached the group. Upon drawing near, Lazaro saw, to both his surprise and dismay, that the wailing was coming from no less than his wife herself who, garbed in the manner and dress of a Chinese courtesan, was on her knees. The people around her appeared to be the creditors that Lazaro had left in China, but their skins were dark blue and they were wearing clothes made from the skins of tigers.

Lazaro's creditors gathered around the woman. One of them held her by her hair, saying that they would let her go if the Sangley gave them what was due to them. Upon hearing this, Lazaro said that he tried to call attention to himself by throwing a stone in their midst. Lazaro's demon creditors all looked towards his direction and the moment they saw him, stared at him in a way that he felt he would melt. The creditors then drew near him, demanding that he speak. However, try as he might, not a word escaped from Lazaro's mouth. Enraged, the creditors threatened to behead his wife if he did not speak, which he was unable to do so no matter how hard he tried. Strangely enough, Lazaro also mentioned that even though he tried his best to speak, he felt that a part of himself was apathetic to the whole situation despite seeing his wife in that manner.

Seeing that Lazaro had, perhaps, no intention of talking, one of the demon creditors drew out his sword and was about to cut his wife's head off when a great rumble was heard and the approach of an army of tens of thousands of soldiers was seen. Lazaro then said that at the sight of the thousands of banners and flags, war chariots, and horsemen, the demon creditors spat at the ground, cursed the heavens, and together with his wife, disappeared into the mist. Just as soon as they were gone, the great army that had put them to fright arrived.

The Sangley said that the army was comprised of frightful-looking soldiers, with their swords drawn and their bows already taut. There were ghosts and the walking dead, with their exposed organs and missing limbs visible, as well as large creatures clad in full battle armour. Among the huge creatures, there was a giant warrior that Lazaro estimated to be over ten feet in height who was seen riding atop a magnificent black stallion. Both the warrior and his horse were clad in gleaming metal armour. Beside the huge creature was a slightly smaller creature, about eight feet in height with the head of an ox.

The huge warrior approached the Sangley and after saying that he was called the General, asked him who he was that dared to remain in his presence. Lazaro tried to speak yet was unable to do so as if his tongue had been cut. In voices that made Lazaro's blood curdle, the ghostly soldiers began clamouring for him to be killed; some said that they wanted to shred him to pieces, while others said that they wanted to shoot an arrow through his heart. Yet, since the Sangley still refused to speak, the General ordered for him to captured and brought before him and the other officers of his army. Lazaro said that he was then bound in chains and led along the barren road to the General's camp.

Upon arriving at the General's camp, Lazaro said that he was brought to one of the gargantuan tents and was told to wait by a soldier who had half of his face torn off to reveal a grinning skull. After a few moments, the General went into the tent, accompanied by the ox-headed creature as well as other monstrosities with the heads of dragons, horses, serpents, and other animals. They were not wearing their armour as they were clad in long, flowing robes and wore hats reserved for high-level mandarins instead of helmets.

According to Lazaro, the General spoke first, saying that the Sangley had to identify himself, else he would be executed on the spot and his body hung up a post to feed the birds. Yet, Lazaro was still unable to utter a word, causing the ghostly soldiers at the entrance of the tent to jeer at him, saying that he should have been killed for his impudence from the very start. In the midst of such a commotion, one of the General's officers, a burly creature with the head of a scorpion, shouted for all to be quiet and said that it had already come to their knowledge that the Sangley was named Tu Tzu-Ch'un—a thief and a heretic who had run away to escape the people that he had defrauded. To this the

General said that the Sangley had to attest to this himself and clapped his hands in such a manner that Lazaro said sounded like thunder. Immediately, Lazaro's wife appeared, still dressed in the manner of a Chinese courtesan. Lazaro said that at the sight of her, he was filled with sorrow but remained unable to speak.

The General then told Lazaro that if he were to continue to remain silent, his wife would die a terrible death. While Lazaro said that he was still unable to talk during this time, part of him felt at ease upon hearing the General's words— as if everything was a dream. Consequently, the General nodded to one of the soldiers at the back, a small demon with the head of a fish, who drew a dagger and tore off the clothes of Lazaro's wife and starting from the woman's feet, began to slowly peel off her skin in thin strips.

As she was being peeled, Lazaro's wife began to scream, curse, and beg for Lazaro to speak. But despite her screams and pleas, he was still unable to utter a word, and stood in front of everything, still silent. By the time the fish-headed soldier had gone to peeling off the skin from the belly of Lazaro's wife, he said that he could hear his wife breathing her last. At that point, the General called attention to the woman's pregnancy, and nodded to the fish-headed soldier, who broke open the thick flesh of Lazaro's wife who, at that moment, expired. The fish-headed creature then reached into the womb of the corpse and pulled the unborn child out with his scaly hands.

Accordingly, the Sangley said that he was both nauseated and wanted to tear his hair out in grief. However, he still remained standing in his place, not a single sound escaping from his mouth. After the fish-headed soldier laid the Sangley's unborn baby on the table in front of the General, the soldier disappeared. In a rage, the General then ordered that the Sangley be kept in a cage outside the tent, until he spoke or his unborn child reached manhood.

Lazaro then said that the General's soldiers locked him up in a cage full of tigers, serpents, scorpions, and fierce lions. However terrifying this may have been, Lazaro said that he was unable to make a sound, and the animals, some of whom even took to leaping over him as well as snapping at him, eventually disappeared. The Sangley then said that hail and rain started to fall as a huge storm suddenly appeared, turning the whole sky black. Whorls of fire encircled Lazaro while at the same time, bolts of lightning began to fall near him. In moments, the waters around him began to reach several feet high, as it seemed like the mountains were beginning to crumble and in the same manner, the land began to break open. The Sangley said that he was so terrified that he tried to keep his eyes closed, yet he did not stir from his place or utter a sound. When everything seemed to come to pass, the General's soldiers came to fetch him and accordingly, led him once more into the tent.

Inside the tent, Lazaro said that almost nothing had changed—the General and his officers were still seated at their place while the ghostly soldiers still stood near the entrance of the tent. However, Lazaro did not see his unborn son. In his stead was a young man with brown skin and a face and mannerisms that Lazaro recognized as his own. Lazaro's son resembled his father in all physical aspects, from his nose to his eyes and mouth, with the exception being his skin, which was that of his mother's. Since the Sangley still remained silent, the General said that if he would not speak, his son would be punished accordingly. After he had uttered his words, the General took a goblet of water and gargled, spitting a dark, red liquid on the ground. The Sangley said that he could see beads of water stuck on the General's thick, long beard.

The General's ghostly soldiers then led Lazaro and his son outside the tent and after stripping the son's garments, tied him to a pole. A fire was then lit around the feet of the Lazaro's son and a soldier with the head of a pigeon drew near, holding an iron rod with a tiger claw attached at its end. With hard strokes, the soldier began hitting the back of Lazaro's son who, despite wincing at every blow, remained as silent as his father. After a few dozen strokes, the soldier stopped and some of the other ghosts brought out two cauldrons—one of black, hot oil and the other brimming with melted bronze.

Untying Lazaro's son from the pole, the soldiers threw him into the cauldron of hot oil. While Lazaro could see the pain on his son's face, the young man remained silent. After a few minutes, the soldiers pulled out the young man from the cauldron. His body, already raw from the beating he took, was burnt black, with some of his limbs appearing cooked to a crisp. The soldiers then dragged his son and put him into the second cauldron. When the soldier pulled him out, Lazaro said that his son looked like a horribly contorted statue, with his charred limbs appearing to have hardened. Lazaro also said that more than his inability to speak, a deep numbness had taken possession of him.

Despite his condition, Lazaro's son was still alive, his burnt and metal-coated chest still rising and falling with his every breath. Seeing this, the soldiers laughed and brought out a box of scorpions, taking turns putting them on the young man's head.

The scorpions dug their stingers in the ears, eyes, and skull of Lazaro's son, who was writhing silently in pain as the soldiers laughed. Lazaro then said that after a few moments, the soldiers brought out a cross that was lacquered bright red and told the young man to carry it and his father to follow. Weakened by his ordeals, Lazaro's son carried the cross while dragging his burnt and heavy legs as the soldiers began to lead both father and son towards a hill full of swords. Lazaro said that he still felt numb, as he followed the soldiers up the hill. He could see a lot of skulls and corpses impaled on the different blades of various sizes and shapes. As Lazaro's son carried the cross, he dragged his legs through the path, the sword blades cutting into his legs so many times that he fell thrice before they reached the top of the hill.

At the summit, the soldiers laid the young man's cross on his back and, after pulling his arms in such a way that his body was in the same manner as that which pinned him, drove huge nails into the cross, right through his hands. Lazaro said that he still could neither feel nor say a thing, as the soldiers broke his son's legs by stomping on his fried, metal-covered limbs. The Sangley also said that he was not able to see his son's face the whole time as the young man was still pinned under his cross.

The soldiers then erected the young man's crucifix upside down, in such a way that the son's head was suspended and his broken limbs dangled in the manner of a puppet. Lazaro said that he could see his son's breath begin to weaken. The ox-headed officer then appeared, bearing an axe that

Lazaro estimated to be fifteen feet in height. Lazaro said that the ox-headed officer wielded the axe with ease, placing the blade near the head of the young man and cleanly severing it from his neck. The head of Lazaro's son rolled on the ground. However, Lazaro said that as it lay on the ground, his son's head suddenly spoke in a voice that was chillingly his own, saying '*Abba, Abba, lem, sabachthani?*' before he breathed his last. At that point, Lazaro said that he had lost consciousness and had once again awakened in his house, his wife tending to his attention.

At the conclusion of Lazaro's account, I had been put in a state of confusion, especially since I had by no means expected such a frightening tale. Since I did not know what to make of Lazaro's story all throughout his narration, I must confess, with some embarrassment, that I had been unable to notice that his hands were unbound and instead of the wounds I had seen a few months before, his palms only had small holes in the middle, with bigger wounds at the back of his hands. I was so distraught with this realization that I left his house immediately and, upon returning to the convent, fell into a state of weeping. For three days, I was in such a state, unable to eat or perform my priestly duties, that the others became worried.

How shall I go about explaining my circumstances during those days? In vain did I try to thrust from my memory the horrors narrated by Lazaro de Chino, for it seemed that these were overwhelming even for one such as myself. In my fear and sorrow, I sought solace and strength from our Lord's experience—His temptation by Satan as well as His passion and death. In the end, the scriptures allowed me to conquer these feelings that, owing to their inherent complexity, I am unable to explain in any words. As a testament to our Lord's power and glory, I resumed my priestly duties after resting for an additional two days. This was a move that proved itself necessary for the trials of the next few days not only saw the Sangleys revolt but also the demise of Lazaro de Chino, his native wife, and unborn son.

As I have already said, on the feast of San Francisco on 3 October, word had spread that the former governor, Don Luis de Dasmariñas had asked Governor Acuña to dispatch soldiers, as it had come to his knowledge that the Sangleys in both Tondo and Binondo had begun to rise in rebellion. Although uncertainty and nervousness were felt throughout the city, it was only between the hours of one and two o' clock in the afternoon that the alarm was sounded, and a state of commotion broke out among the city's inhabitants owing to the small number of our countrymen in these islands. Accordingly, the walls of the city were manned. However, due to the aforementioned shortage of men—both soldiers and those of other occupations, it was decided that the clergy would also take part in the defence of the city. Owing to the malady that I had just experienced, it was agreed that I would serve as a watchman, being unable to effectively use musket, pike, or sword.

Positioned at the top of the city walls, I could see the Sangleys, in their frenzy, setting fire to everything in their path. I must admit that despite the tumultuous circumstances of those moments, I was bothered by the thought that among the Sangleys responsible for the carnage below, were those whose needs Padre Gonzales and I have sought to answer over the past few months. The Lord have mercy on their souls. The attack from the Sangleys commenced in a few hours, with members of the clergy helping to keep the Sangleys at bay—one of the order of San Francisco, a former soldier, proved himself with valorous deeds brought by his skill in musketry. Eventually, the Sangleys were forced to retire, retreating to the outskirts of the city as well as the surrounding provinces, where they were eventually routed by our forces.

It was only after the revolt had been quelled that I was able to hear about the events and battles that followed after the Sangleys had been repulsed by our efforts, such as the capture and execution of the traitor Juan Bautista de Vera, whose claims disavowing any role in the revolt were not taken seriously. His properties were confiscated and his lands sprinkled with salt. However, as you must have heard about these, since many reports detailing these events have been sent to Spain, I will not delve into such things anymore. Likewise, it was only after the uprising that I learned of the death of Lazaro de Chino, as well as his wife and unborn child during the first days of the revolt.

According to several eyewitnesses, mostly neighbours of Lazaro who also worked with him, on the morning of 3 October, Lazaro was quarrying stone for his work on a statue commissioned by our archbishop for the upcoming feast of the Immaculate Conception. While it was apparent that all the Sangleys knew about the planned uprising, some chose to ignore the call to arms made by their countrymen, opting instead to stay home, with some even having enough courage to continue practising their trade. As such, these eyewitnesses said that at around 10.00 a.m., while most of their countrymen were already outside the city walls, Lazaro was working in the quarry when a seraphic apparition of no less than San Francisco made itself visible. Accordingly, the men stopped working, with some of them fleeing in fright and the others, who were too stunned to do likewise, remaining in their positions, unable to move. It is said that upon seeing the Holy Father San Francisco, who was around forty feet in height, Lazaro was also struck dumb and remained in his place. According to the eyewitnesses, Lazaro did not offer any resistance when San Francisco held him by the neck with hands that they said also bore the marks of our Lord, as these people were among those who had originally reported to de Vera about Lazaro's condition. It is said that the saint then strangled Lazaro, who expired within seconds, his body bursting into flames as San Francisco released him from his grip, whereupon the apparition vanished, leaving behind a pile of charred bones that had been Lazaro de Chino only moments before. The eyewitnesses said that they fled soon after, as they were terrified by the event that they had just witnessed.

I also learned from others that were familiar with Lazaro's family that coincidentally, Lazaro's pregnant wife also left the realm of the living during the revolt, this time on the second day, 4 October. According to witnesses, at around 1.00 p.m., after the attack of the Sangleys was repulsed by the defenders of the city, some of the Sangleys in Binondo, who were sympathetic to their countrymen's endeavours, chose to join the revolt. Since the family of Lazaro de Chino was known among his people as sympathetic to the Crown of Spain, a group of Christian Sangleys went to his house, wherein Lazaro's wife, who was already in her final month of pregnancy, was resting. Being vagabonds with nothing to lose, these Sangleys sealed the house by barricading it, after which they set the house on fire from all directions, burning both Lazaro's wife and unborn baby as they razed the house to the ground.

With the news of the strange circumstances of Lazaro de Chino's death, as well as the unfortunate murder of his family by several of his countrymen, I found it interesting to hear reports that the Holy Father San Francisco was also seen atop the city walls while we were defending the city, killing the Sangleys who had tried to scale the walls as the crucified image of our Lord dripped blood above, something that I am unable to account for, as I did not see such a thing although I was present there. However, it is true that despite their superior numbers, the Sangleys did indeed become disheartened after trying in vain to breach our defences. This leads me to wonder whether our miraculous victory can indeed be attributed to such a marvellous event and whether Francisco appeared above the city walls after taking care of the account of Lazaro de Chino. Yet, I must confess that the reasons for the death of Lazaro de Chino, as well as the apparent miracles that he had shown and told me about, still lie beyond my comprehension, especially since it has been unanimously attested that the Sangley was exemplary in his deeds and actions as a Christian. I believe that to these questions, no answers on this land will ever be found. However, let this account be a testament to the wondrous events that surrounded Lazaro de Chino's life and death. May the Lord have mercy on his soul!

Doubtless, you have read the manuscript I have prepared—before you course it to the Brothers de Joya, please do an honour to my person by placing it under your scrutiny for any errors in language that I may have committed. As I think about everything in the manuscript, the words of our Lord ring clear in my heart. Truly He is the way, the truth, and the life! Despite the experiences that I have had with the Sangleys, I remain confident that the Lord's words will eventually reach them as a people. We must not assume that the Sangleys will remain forever blind and deaf to our Lord's message, them being a people who, despite their shortcomings, remain industrious and smart. I can only hope that there will come a day wherein we would be able to preach to the Sangleys in their own land so that there will be Chinese ministries and churches in the future. I believe that help must be accorded to them so that not only would they be able to help themselves but others as well. For this reason, I believe that what the order has been doing in these islands with regards to the Sangleys is for the best.

Since you know the people who I am acquainted with, I also ask of you to greet them in my name. Tell them that I am doing well despite having encountered things that my priestly training had not prepared me for, inasmuch as both Padre Gonzales and myself have made great strides in our work with the Sangleys, who have been growing in number despite the thousands that perished during the uprising and its aftermath, as the junks have once again begun to arrive over the past few weeks. The Lord have mercy on us, as we strive to compel them to hear His Word, not just for their sake, but for the sake of all humanity as well.

(In the city of Manila, on 13 June,
in the year of our Lord 1604)
Padre Tomas Rodriguez

Where Old Whores Go to Die

Jahannam Agency for International Aid Small Grants Programme (SGP) Project Appraisal Form

1. **Country:**
   Philippines
2. **Project Title:**
   Dama de Noche Rehabilitation and Realignment Community
3. **Project Location:**
   P. Damaso St, Barangay Lazaro de Chino, Manila, NCR
4. **Project Sector:**
   Human Resource Standardization
5. **Project Duration:**
   One Year
6. **Budget:**
   Amount Requested: ₱1,357,390
   Counterpart: ₱1,456,334
   Total: ₱2,813,724

7. **Recipient Organization:**

Emancipation from Structural Malaise Foundation, Inc.

Contact Person: Ms Ligaya Cononegra

                   Executive Director

Address: Head Office, Dama de Noche Rehabilitation and

              Realignment Community Complex, P. Damaso

              St, Barangay Lazaro de Chino, Manila, NCR

Telephone: (632) 556-99876

Email: lcononegra@esmf.org

8. **Organizational Assessment:**

The Emancipation from Structural Malaise Foundation, Inc. (ESMF) is a non-stock, non-profit organization (NPO) dedicated to alleviating the plight of those severely affected by structural inequality. As such, it aims to conceptualize, execute, and sustain projects and programmes that would effectively negate the physical and psychological effects of structural inequality among marginal groups and help them conform to international human resource productivity standards.

Since its registration with the Securities and Exchange Commission in 2008, ESMF and its staff of seventy professionals has been involved in the conceptualization and undertaking of different programmes that satisfy its purposive and functional thrusts. The organization, from the beginning, has maintained its flagship programme, the Dama de Noche Rehabilitation and Realignment Community to provide prostitutes over the age of forty with the opportunity to realign their position as human resources, as well as to be remembered upon reaching mortality.

Additionally, ESMF has also linked and developed working partnerships with various organizations and agencies to create collaborative programmes. Aside from being tapped as a resource partner by the International Committee on Children's Rights for the Southeast Asian leg of its visiting exhibition, the organization has also received funding and support from the Gehenna Fund, the Naraka Institute, the Di Yu International Cooperation Agency, and the Sheol Fund for Human Resource Development. Among ESMF's projects and programmes are Acculturation and Standardization Facilities in Ifugao, Mindoro, Davao Oriental, Sultan Kudarat, and Sulu; Epidermis Bleaching and Rhinoplasty Missions in Agta and Aeta communities; and a Happiness Reeducation Centre for sharecroppers in Negros Occidental, which is incidentally, presently receiving assistance from the Jahannam Agency for International Aid's (JAIA) Small Grants Programme.

9. **Project Background:**

While the problem of aged prostitutes can be said to be as old as the profession itself, the demographic trend in the past few years has shown a marked increase in their numbers, mostly due to the inadequate replenishment of the younger generation in the turnover cycle, as well as the influx of provincial old maids into urban areas brought upon by the government's diversification programme of the mid-1990s. According to the Ministry of Statistics (MOS), the national percentage of prostitutes over the age of forty rose from 3.5 per cent in 1990 to 9.78 per cent in 2005. Consequently, the Bureau of Brothels and Freelance Prostitutes (BOBFP) reports that the number of non-earning and low-earning prostitutes rose from 5.23 per cent to 15.9 per cent during the same period.

Following the Philippines' ratification of the International Convention on the Productivity of Human Resources in 2007, several civil society personalities organized a summit to discuss ways to help the country conform to international standards, especially with respect to marginal groups. Because of the alarming statistics from the MOS and BOBFP, the prevalence of highly publicized incidents involving customer rejection of aged prostitutes in several Manila massage parlours, and the increasing number of unclaimed corpses of aged prostitutes in morgues, aged prostitution was considered a priority sector during the summit.

The summit was held from 20–21 June 2007. In response to the realization that the government was too ill-equipped to facilitate a transition to international human resource standards, a resolution was passed at the termination of the summit detailing the need for a concerted effort on the part of civil society to bridge this gap. Consequently, the ESMF was organized from the ranks of the summit participants.

During the formulation of the ESMF's organizational structure, vision-mission-objectives, and by-laws, it was decided that the critical nature of the problem concerning aged prostitutes necessitated an immediate intervention. Accordingly, it was determined that the organization's initial flagship programme would be one addressing aged prostitutes, with other sectors such as indigenous people and landless rural workers being targeted through smaller initiatives.

Shortly after its registration with the Securities and Exchange Commission, the organization purchased a two-hectare lot from the local administrative body of Manila with assistance from the Sheol Fund for Human Resource Development. Part of what used to be the Manila Theological Institute, the lot has now become the present site of the Dama de Noche Rehabilitation and Realignment Community Complex.

Although the community has been operating successfully for the past four years, the organization recognizes that there is a need for additional capacity building initiatives to ensure the maintenance and continued innovation of the project's different components while providing the possibility of its replication in other parts of the country. It is in this respect that it is requesting assistance from the Jahannam Agency for International Aid to strengthen and sustain the community's growth and possible replication in the future.

10. Project Description:

As its name suggests, the Dama de Noche Rehabilitation and Realignment Community seeks to rehabilitate aged prostitutes into productive human resources. Located in a two-hectare site that also houses the offices of the ESMF, the community revolves around a sequential order of processes that are conducted in segregated areas within the complex.

The initial process starts when the beneficiaries reach the community grounds. Upon their disembarkation from the ESMF service vehicles, beneficiaries are led to the Reception Area, where their garments are removed and collected for incineration, and their faces and bodies rinsed of any cosmetics. This is to ensure that some of the extraneous elements that they may bring with them are not brought into the community. The beneficiaries are then shown to the Reception Hall, where they are issued standardized smocks and slippers. They are then led to their quarters, which are located at the sides of the hall. Each beneficiary is assigned to a corresponding room, equipped with a cot, a latrine, and adequate water and provisions. In order to make sure that the beneficiaries become familiar with themselves, each room and piece of furniture is covered by mirrors or a similarly reflective substance.

After inhabiting their quarters for a week, the beneficiaries are then brought to the External Rehabilitation Facility for the second process. Before they enter the facility, their bodies are washed to remove any sweat and grime that may have accumulated over the course of the week. They are then anesthetized and brought into the facility on stretchers.

The beneficiaries then undergo a series of surgical procedures that are meant to further their rehabilitation. Building on the results achieved in the initial process, eligible beneficiaries first have glycolic acid tattooed over corresponding areas to remove any extrinsic elements. Subsequently, they are subject to a hymenoplasty (in cases where this is not applicable, an appropriate substitute is created and applied), in addition to a sealing of their labium using sterilized twine, while leaving a small gap for urination. Although seemingly contradictory, the first procedure is meant to physically rehabilitate the beneficiaries while the second seeks to eliminate an inutile source of livelihood. In a parallel manner, missing teeth are replaced by plastic imitations, after which beneficiaries' mouths are wired shut. To facilitate the flow of nourishment, an incision is made and a feeding tube inserted into their stomachs.

Following these procedures, beneficiaries are brought to the facility's ward to recuperate. Starting from this point, until near the termination of their stay in the community, they are given a constant supply of sedatives.

Once the one-month recuperation period has elapsed, beneficiaries are moved to the Internal Rehabilitation Facility for the third process. After their smocks, slippers, and feeding tubes are removed, and bandages applied over their stomach incisions, the beneficiaries are brought into the facility's communal shower area, where they are subject to three cycles of varying concentrations of a primarily trigesterone biphosphate-based compound to stimulate their internal rehabilitation.

The first cycle is meant to cleanse the beneficiaries of any spiritual residue left by their past customers by removing the motivations for their engaging of beneficiary services. This means that the accrued layers of motives such as the different forms and combinations of customer lust, boredom, loneliness, anger, distraction searching, and curiosity are washed away, regardless of whether the beneficiaries are aware of their existence.

After the first cycle, beneficiaries are dried to prevent the different concentrations of chemicals from mixing.

The second cycle, which aims to rid beneficiaries of their different responsibilities, is then commenced. This takes away whatever sense of duty they may have had in continuing to engage in a profession that has become misaligned with their present human resource capabilities. In this respect, their duties to themselves, their families, and other social obligations are extinguished.

Upon the completion of the second cycle and the drying of the beneficiaries, the third cycle is started. Meant to remove any self-delusions about their value, this cycle negates the propensity of beneficiaries to attach any form of material value to their services. Once this is accomplished, bandages are then removed, feeding tubes reinserted, and the beneficiaries are clothed in their smocks and slippers.

Unlike the first two processes, beneficiaries are not expected to remain in the facility once the third process is over, since they are now considered fully rehabilitated. Thus, they are immediately transferred to the Handicraft and Living Centre for the fourth process.

Aside from housing their quarters, the Handicraft and Living Centre is where the rehabilitated beneficiaries are realigned. Through the centre's in-house handicraft production facility, ESMF staff help beneficiaries conform to international human resource productivity standards by retrieving hair and fingernails from them. These are then processed into a variety of exportable handicrafts such as oil mops, garments, and costume jewellery.

Understandably, the length of stay of each beneficiary in the centre varies, depending on the onset of the first signs of mortality. Ranging from a few days to months, or even years, the initial indications of resource degradation signify that a particular beneficiary can no longer continue living in the centre. At this point, the beneficiary is transferred to the Mortality House for the fifth process.

In contrast to the other areas in the community, beneficiaries stationed at the Mortality House are not subject to any intervention. Composed of a two-storey structure equipped with standardized cubicles, the Mortality House was created in order to facilitate the progression of beneficiaries towards mortality. In line with this, feeding tubes are removed and sedatives are withheld. The beneficiaries are then secured in their respective cubicles, where they are kept until mortality is reached.

The final process begins once mortality is reached. Upon beneficiary retrieval from the Mortality House, their remains are brought back to the Handicraft and Living Centre. There, smocks and slippers are collected for future use, skins are peeled for tanning, organs are ground for livestock feed, and bones are cleaned and reassembled for sale to medical institutions.

11. Beneficiaries

Beneficiaries are selected by the ESMF through the members of its Disguised Selection Group (DSG), who are essentially disguised individuals tasked to determine the capacity of a prostitute to continue being a productive human resource. Because of the numbered board system prevalent in low-end massage parlours, such as the House of the Rising Sun and Roxanne's Health

Club, DSG members adopt a random number method to find aged prostitutes in these places. Conversely, they also periodically go around Manila's streets to identify prospective beneficiaries from the city's numerous streetwalkers.

Once a prospective beneficiary has been identified, the DSG member uses an SMS message to notify his companions, who immediately come to help secure the prospect into awaiting ESMF service vehicles. When service vehicles have reached their full capacity, potential beneficiaries are brought to ESMF Holding Centres, where the DSG convenes to reach a consensus on prospective admission into the community.

While the determination of the income-generating potential of prostitutes is subjective and therefore arbitrary, the multifaceted make-up of the DSG allows them to determine whether a prostitute has become an idle resource, even among those with gerontophilia. In this sense, although there have been instances of beneficiaries under the age of forty, their rehabilitation and realignment are justified inasmuch as their lack of utility has been established by the DSG. As such, once consensus has been reached, selected beneficiaries are brought to the community, while those not selected are returned to where they were found.

At present, the community has hosted 160 beneficiaries. Of these, twenty-seven have already finished staying in the Mortality House, while the rest are presently undergoing the various other processes. Coming from different parts of Manila, the beneficiaries are evenly distributed between low-end massage parlour attendants and freelance prostitutes. However, there seems to be a trend towards an increasing number of aged freelance prostitutes. This is due to the increasing influx of provincial old maids into Manila, as well as the significant number of aged massage parlour attendants rounded up in the first few searches of the finite number of the city's low-end massage parlours, which have since tried to conform to international human resource standards to avoid further operational disruptions.

Although the community has managed to help a significant number of old prostitutes, it is apparent that its potential has not fully been realized. According to MOS and BOBFP statistics, as of January 2012, the percentage of Manila prostitutes over the age of forty and the number of non-earning and low-earning prostitutes stands at 8.45 per cent and 14.2 per cent, respectively. While this may be seen as a welcome development, their continued statistical significance, coupled with ever-increasing figures from provincial cities, make the case for the community's continued improvement and eventual replication.

12. Project Assistance Components:

As part of its efforts to further its capacity building initiatives for its flagship project, the ESMF would like to request JAIA for assistance in the continued improvement of the Dama de Noche Rehabilitation and Realignment Community based on gaps identified in the community's different areas during its four years of existence.

Firstly, the ESMF would like to request JAIA's help in procuring unbreakable reflective substances for the

Reception Hall quarters. Over the past few years, the constant thrashing of the beneficiaries has shattered the mirrors of their assigned quarters. Aside from minimizing the risk of self-inflicted injury, the use of unbreakable reflective substances will also be cost-effective, since the replacement of mirrors with every new batch of beneficiaries has proven to be an unnecessary expense.

Additionally, funding is also needed for the conduct of security training for ESMF personnel assigned at the External Rehabilitation Facility. This is because of several incidents concerning beneficiaries trying to escape as they are transferred from their Reception Hall quarters. Although the ESMF staff has always managed to retrieve these errant beneficiaries, their stubborn refusal to accept their present situation has done nothing but delay the second process.

In order to further minimize other sources of process delays, assistance is also needed for the drainage enlargement of the Internal Rehabilitation Facility. Since each chemical cycle takes a while to fully drain out, beneficiaries are often left standing for two hours between each cycle, even after they are already dried and readied. Although their sedated state ensures that they cause no inconvenience, the minimization of this wait time would enable beneficiaries to be transferred earlier to the Handicraft and Living Centre, where their productive lives start.

On this note, it is also requested that a series of skills training seminars be given to ESMF staff assigned at the Handicraft and Living Centre's different handicraft facilities. These skills involve not only product design and creation but also human farming, since hair and fingernail wastage were found to be common problems during the organization's most recent internal assessment.

The ESMF staff at the centre's different handicraft facilities would also greatly benefit from the reduction of external nuisances. As such, JAIA's assistance would also be solicited for soundproofing the Mortality House. This is because despite the Mortality House being located a kilometre away, the screams and wails of cubicle-bound beneficiaries have managed to reach the centre, effectively lowering staff morale and causing further inefficiency.

13. Project Sustainability:

In four years of existence, the Dama de Noche Rehabilitation and Realignment Community has proven itself to be a financially soluble enterprise. This can be attributed to the strength of the pre-and-post-mortality products produced at the Handicraft and Living Centre, which have managed to more than adequately address operation expenditures.

Aside from being based on regenerative sources, the different products produced before the beneficiaries are brought into the Mortality House have proven to have international appeal. For example, the hair acquired from beneficiaries has been made into oil mops, wigs, and garments that have been exported to numerous overseas markets. In particular, the international growth of oil refineries and the subsequent increase in oil spills have proven to be a lucrative source of income. Owing to a scarcity of oil-absorbent materials, global demand for oil mops has been high, with the community-produced ones gaining a substantial market share over the past few years.

Much like the oil mops, wigs, and garments, brushes produced from the stubble of beneficiaries after they are rendered bald, as well as costume jewellery made from fingernails have also been exported overseas.

In contrast, products produced from the remains of beneficiaries mostly serve the domestic market, although some accessories made from beneficiary leather have been exported. In this sense, community-produced livestock feed has been used extensively in the central Luzon and southern Tagalog regions, while the reassembled skeletons have found a place in the medical departments of Manila's universities.

14. **Project Management:**

Management of the Dama de Noche Rehabilitation and Realignment Community is undertaken by the ESMF Secretariat in close coordination with its Board of Directors. Headed by its Executive Director, the different members of the ESMF Secretariat are responsible for the day-to-day operations of the community (see attached organizational chart and ESMF constitution for more details).

15. **Assistance Implementation Schedule:**

See attached document

16. **Cost and Financing:**

See attached document

17. **Recommendations and Justifications:**

It is recommended that the proposed assistance be given by the JAIA's Small Grants Programme, since:

a. Human Resource Standardization is one of the priority areas for JAIA in its Philippine Strategy Plan for 2010–2016.

b. It falls within the jurisdiction of the programme's mandate of providing infrastructural improvements and technical assistance to worthy NPO projects.

c. It is a low-risk endeavour given the ESMF's proven track record with JAIA's SGP in the Negros Occidental Happiness Reeducation Centre, and that the community has proven itself to be financially sustainable over its four years of existence.

d. Given the project's existing sustainability, the proposed assistance would serve to catalyse the processing of beneficiaries, which will subsequently pave the way for the project's replication in the long-term, effectively giving a chance for utility to be derived from old prostitutes, not just in Manila but all over the Philippines as well.

Appraised by: Monique Sim-Francia
            Programme Officer
            Small Grants Programme
            Jahannam Agency for International
            Aid, Manila

The Way of Those Who Stayed Behind

Last year, as you may remember, I was unable to go to Edmonton for the annual CIPA conference due to the abrupt death of my great-grandmother. I never would have imagined that my first trip back to Manila would be for a funeral, especially after having been gone for so long. I also didn't expect that I would be going back alone, since I had been meaning to schedule a family vacation to the Philippines over the past couple of years.

In some ways, though, I was relieved that Miriam had an urgent board meeting on her pet project and that the kids were in the middle of their finals. Although I would have wanted the kids to meet their relatives, I was a bit hesitant to have them accompany me on this trip. Since a lot of changes have surely happened over the years, I certainly didn't want to disappoint them about how different Manila was from all the stories that I had told them. Besides, their presence would have hindered me from making an inventory of family assets—something that occurred to me once the initial shock at hearing about Tai Ma's death had worn off. I guess all the horror stories about family members suing each other must have gotten to me, and I figured that it would be in the best interest of my family to know and protect our entitlements, especially with both my parents dead for over twenty years.

And so, shortly after the funeral and a couple of days before my flight back, I visited the old family compound in Pasay. To nip any suspicions about my visit—to what I heard was an otherwise idle property that had been unofficially turned into a storehouse even while Tai Ma was still alive—in the bud, I had told my Grand Uncle Victor that I wanted to look for some old personal items to ship back to Vancouver.

I was nervous as the car made its way past the sprawling Dama de Noche Centre and into the almost unbearably dirty and cramped side streets of Pasay. Although I was going back to the scene of some of my more memorable childhood memories, I felt like I was going to an unfamiliar, potentially inhospitable place. Save for my belief that I would be able to find the documents I needed, I hardly knew what to expect.

All these inutile, meandering thoughts disappeared as the driver stopped at a familiar, tall, brown gate. After a few moments, a shabbily dressed guard drew open the gates to a driveway that I hadn't seen since I lived in the compound.

It had been nearly two decades since the abduction of my cousin Raul brought to a close the month that had already seen the high-profile death of Charlene Mayne Sy during a botched rescue attempt. And, while Raul was released unharmed after a couple of days (and around $15,000), the shock of the whole incident prompted Miriam and I to seriously consider starting our family in a less hostile environment. Canada had just relaxed its immigration policies a couple of years before, and as a matter of course, quickly made its way to the top of our options. Surprisingly, our idea was received well by the family, with Tai Ma even saying that it was a golden opportunity for childless newlyweds still searching for their way in life. Consequently, by the middle of the following month, we arrived in Vancouver, where we eventually gained citizenship, had children and made a name for ourselves in our respective fields. In the same way that Miriam worked herself up the corporate ladder from secretary to executive, the postgraduate degree that I pursued upon reaching Canada eventually led to my present post as an adjunct professor of Political Anthropology.

I was still thinking about these life changes as I stepped out of the car and onto the sloping driveway of the main house. Looking around, I could see that the compound had also changed over the years. Aside from an apparent need for immediate renovation, the buildings seemed smaller and more crowded, while the garden playground where my cousins and I used to play had fallen into the trappings of disuse, with its slides and swings rusted and bent beyond normal repair. Perhaps the most noticeable change was the presence of what appeared to be a small, brightly painted Chinese temple in the deepest area of the compound, right on the spot where my Aunt Raquel's (Raul's mother) house should have stood. A concrete wall with a small gate was now located on the path that had led to Aunt Raquel's house.

The new structure made me uncomfortable. While the funeral had some of the usual Chinese rituals such as the burning of a paper house, money, and cars, and the placing of chicken's blood on Tai Ma's portrait, all this had occurred after the requiem mass. As far as I knew, we had all been raised as Catholics. Even Tai Ma had been baptized, although

I must admit that I remember her seemingly making small paper birds fly by chanting what sounded like gibberish, aside from spending hours staring at a porcelain bowl filled with water.

I was so preoccupied with the small temple that I was startled by a voice that said the family would regularly pray there on Sundays. Turning around, I found myself in front of a nondescript, middle-aged man who introduced himself as the caretaker.

After mentioning that Grand Uncle Victor had called him about my visit, the caretaker said that he had been surprised when he learned about my existence because he thought that he had met the whole family throughout his decade of employment. Although I found his statement odd, since it was hardly plausible that I was never mentioned in ten years, I decided that it barely warranted a response. However, as he fumbled with the keys, I asked him when the last members of the family had left the compound.

The caretaker replied that Grand Uncle Victor's family had moved out sometime during the previous year, a few months before the sudden decline of Tai Ma's health. He added that while Tai Ma's age had always been a cause for concern, her abrupt illness and death had caught them all by surprise. Finally finding the right key and opening the door, the caretaker wondered aloud what he and the other members of the household help would do now that the family matriarch had passed away.

I kept silent as I entered. I didn't know what to say and felt that my transient status hardly gave me the authority to speak on such matters. Aside from this, I was bothered by the caretaker's use of the Chinese word for matriarch when he referred to Tai Ma. Although we had never called her that, I had heard it used a few times by my relatives during the wake and funeral—something that I just thought to be some sort of new convention.

My silence probably made the caretaker realize that I wasn't there to fraternize with him, since he excused himself after a few moments.

As I walked around, I noticed that things were actually better than what I had expected. True, the house was a bit dusty and some of the rooms were filled with boxes and scattered medical equipment, old appliances, and various knick-knacks, but its main areas were generally clean. It was clear that Tai Ma had given permission for the rest of the family to store their belongings in some of the infrequently used rooms. In this sense, the layout had been mostly unchanged, I noted as I made my way past the plaques and trophies that were still displayed in the small anteroom and through the living room with its clunky big screen TV and huge vases, while sneaking a peek at the dining room before moving up the stairs to the more private areas of the house.

The first thing I noticed when I went up to the second floor was that the bookcases were still in the corner of the main corridor, all of them full of crumbling volumes and ledgers that were propped up by a couple dozen bookends. As you probably expect, I felt compelled to take a look although I was certain that they contained none of the documents I hoped to find. I knew that I was alone and since time was hardly a concern, I could even browse through some of the Chinese texts if I wished.

I went through the contents of the bookshelves methodically. Although the books had always appeared haphazardly and asymmetrically ordered, with some even placed with their spines towards the insides of the shelves, it soon became apparent that someone had put a lot of time and effort in thematically organizing the bookshelves. I guess this explained the numerous bookends and why some of the shelves were only half full. Reading materials on history were divided by subsections relating to time and location, while production books were ordered according to each production phase. Since everything was ordered in such a coherent manner, I was a bit taken aback when I saw a small, handbound volume with a crude drawing of a man seated in a lotus position wedged in between a couple of stained Fujianese cookbooks.

I was immediately drawn to the book, which bore, in bold Chinese characters, the title *The Righteous Way of Heaven in Tumultuous Times*. Looking at the inside cover, I became even more excited when I read that it was produced in 1989 by the Righteous Way of the Loyal Children of Heaven Society.

During my first few years in Vancouver, I would hear rumours within the Chinese–Filipino community about the resurgence of several groups in Manila that claimed to be the successors of old Mainland secret sects such as the White Lotus Society and the Heaven and Earth Society. Rumour had it that at the height of the kidnapping terror, when armed bodyguards had proven themselves useless, and people started to realize that avoiding public places was not a deterrent, the teachings of these groups played a part in strangely aborted abduction attempts. There was talk about a family pre-empting a kidnapping by using what was called a karma mirror, while it was also said that another family had spontaneously brought back a kidnapped son by moving a

small effigy of the boy along a table. Even stranger was the
talk about would-be kidnappers being attacked by little paper
figures before they could complete their plans.

With these thoughts still lingering in my mind, I began
to leaf through the book, even before I sat down on the
chair at the far corner of the corridor. Despite my less-than-
stellar grasp of written Chinese, I was surprised at the speed
and ease with which I went through the text. It was as if
I instantly recognized and understood every character, which
gave me the freedom to occasionally reflect as I read.

The book began with the near-death experience of Jade,
a Fujianese village girl, who, upon regaining consciousness,
finds herself in a vast palace where the ground is made out
of gold and where there appears to be an infinite variety of
pavilions, halls, and terraces bordered by clear streams and
pools. Although amazed by her otherworldly surroundings,
Jade is unable to explore the palace because right in front of
her is an immense golden lotus with an extraordinarily tall old
woman with a kind, sad face is seated in the middle.

At this point the text shifted into verse as the old woman
introduces herself as the Eternal Venerable Mother, who had
given birth to the first man and woman and had sent mankind
to populate the Eastern world. There, her children have lost
their original nature as they learned to immerse themselves in
vanity and avarice. This has been a cause of great suffering for
the Eternal Venerable Mother, whose weeping and imploring
letters have gone unheeded.

The prose portion of the text then resumed, with the
Eternal Venerable Mother telling Jade that she has wanted
nothing more than for her children to return to their native
land in the Original Home in the World of True Emptiness

and be reunited with her on the golden lotus throne. Despite her unnoticed tears and the underwhelming response to her pleas, she has always been hopeful that this reunion will take place. This hope has led her to send messengers to reign and preach the true dharma throughout the three *kalpas* or stages of time. The first messenger was the Lamp-lighting Buddha, who reigned from a five-leafed azure lotus throne throughout his kalpa, which lasted for 108,000 years. He was then followed by Sakyamuni Buddha, the present messenger, who sits on a seven-leafed red lotus throne. While the first two messengers have brought about the repentance of some, the vast majority of people continued to live in sin as the true dharma has gradually given way to the false dharma. This meant that the present kalpa was about to end. The 27,000-year-reign of Sakyamuni Buddha would soon be over, and the Maitreya Buddha, the final messenger, will arrive to begin his time on the nine-leafed white lotus throne.

The Eternal Venerable Mother then tells Jade why she has been summoned to the golden lotus throne. As in the past, the turning of the kalpa would bring forth death and chaos as the present world order is destroyed by successive waves of calamities. Because only the followers of the true dharma will be able to live and prosper during these times, it is imperative that people prepare for the coming of the Maitreya. According to the Eternal Venerable Mother, the quality of Jade's accumulated merit has placed her under the divine grace of heaven. Consequently, she has been chosen to oversee the preparations for the Maitreya's arrival.

The Eternal Venerable Mother then asks Jade if she wishes to accept this responsibility. Jade agrees without hesitation, and the Eternal Venerable Mother proceeds to teach her the secrets to the salvation of mankind. These secrets form the basis of the Righteous Way of the Loyal Children of Heaven Society, which was founded by Jade when she returned to earth and adopted the title of Grand Matriarch of the Righteous Way, which has since been handed down to the eldest daughter in each generation of her descendants.

Although I should have hardly been surprised by this hereditary title, it was suspicious to read it in the book after hearing a shorter version of it being used to refer to Tai Ma over the past few days. As much as I knew that it would be premature to reach any definite conclusions, it was hard not to connect the title with the things that I have encountered.

These things were not only limited to my experiences during this trip. Aside from the presence of the temple and the fact that such a book had been hidden inside the house, I couldn't help but remember what Tai Ma was like. While she certainly had her warm moments, she sometimes carried herself with an air of aloofness that I had always attributed to the language barrier. She seemed to place importance in setting aside a few hours of the day for herself. When my mom was still alive, she would scold me for sneaking into Tai Ma's room, where there was always a stash of assorted cookies, during these quiet afternoons. Although I quickly learned to avoid Tai Ma's room during those times, I remember catching brief glances of her making her little flying birds of paper or seeing her place burned scraps of paper in bottles of water to make the Chinese medicine that would be given to us whenever we got sick. We never really knew if the medicine was effective, since it was always given to us to drink when we were at the tail end of our antibiotic cycle. However, I was intrigued by the flying paper birds, which

I never really understood, since my attempts to bring them up with Tai Ma were constantly met with harsh chastisement—something that caused me to think that it was always her time of the month, although she was probably a couple of decades into her menopause then.

It was difficult to think about all this. As ludicrous as it was to consider that my family was somehow involved in the Righteous Way of the Loyal Children of Heaven Society, or had perhaps, even founded and propagated the sect over generations, I could not help but dwell on the possibilities. If there was some kind of involvement then not only was Tai Ma concealing the truth from me all these years but the other members of the family had also been aware of the sect and had perhaps even participated in its activities. What else could have reasonably explained the presence of the temple? Despite Tai Ma's clout, I doubt that Aunt Raquel would've readily agreed to have the house that she had inherited replaced by such a structure if she didn't approve of it. It was also impossible for anyone in the family to not know about the temple once it had been constructed. Besides, the caretaker did say that they worshipped there every Sunday.

I tried to keep these thoughts in check before they could get any more complicated. I knew that my long absence had hampered my ability to understand the situation in Manila, and that there were other explanations aside from my deliberate exclusion from such an important family matter. Besides, there were too many fundamental things that I didn't know, the most important, perhaps, being actual information about the sect. Save for that pseudohistorical origin story, I knew nothing about the beliefs and activities of the Righteous Way of the Loyal Children of Heaven

Society. This made it hard to prove any relationship between the sect and my family, despite the link that I suspected. Even Tai Ma's actions did not mean anything, however weird they may have been.

Without anyone to talk to, I knew that I could only find the answers I sought in the book. Immersing myself in the next few pages, I gradually noticed that the next nine short chapters were written using the same basic formula.

Following the prose–verse–prose structure of the origin story, the nine chapters focused on the Maitreya Buddha's messages to specific groups of people who will become gravely affected by the turning of the kalpa.

Each of the chapters began with the Maitreya opening the Book of Heaven to look at the state of the world. In what was probably a good indication of the sect's intended audience, the Maitreya's attention was curiously limited to the spread of the false dharma in the Philippines during the early 1990s, with the Book of Heaven showing the misdeeds of each group of people destined to suffer the most at the end of the present kalpa.

After the Maitreya recites a litany of sins attributable to each group, the way towards redemption would then be explained in what I understood to be the sect's basic teachings. Aside from the obvious demand to cease these immoral activities, the Maitreya also called for abstinence from meat, gambling, and alcohol. The Righteous Way also involved the strengthening of the mind and body by the cultivation of *chi* through meditation and exercise. While the physical exercises were only discussed in general terms throughout the nine chapters, meditation was sometimes mentioned with the memorization of what was called the 'Wordless True

Sutra'. This was composed of eight characters that translate as 'Eternal Venerable Mother in Our Original Home in the World of True Emptiness'. Salvation would be achieved through the regular chanting of this sutra and the faithful observance of the Righteous Way, which would enable a repentant sinner to gain enough merit for a place within the protective walls of Cloud City when the kalpa ends.

In contrast, the rejection of the Righteous Way would have dire consequences, as non-believers would suffer, starting with the string of calamities that herald the turning of the kalpa. These initial calamities were alluded to in some chapters as 'the darkness and gunfire amid the loosening of the earth and the storm of flames'—a phrase that was especially chilling for someone who lived in the Philippines during the early 1990s. This made it even more difficult to comprehend the scale and scope of the suffering that will supposedly be sent by the Eternal Venerable Mother as mankind's final punishment for refusing salvation.

According to the book, the final punishment of those who reject the Righteous Way will begin when the true dharma is finally extinguished. Shortly after all the true scriptures vanish from the world, the course of the sun and moon will be altered, and the climate will change abruptly. This cosmic imbalance will be followed by extreme calamities as earth, wind, fire, and water are thrown into chaos, destroying all crops and leaving scores of corpses to rot. A black wind will then blow through the world to reduce all surviving non-believers into piles of white bones and pools of blood.

The mass holocaust of non-believers and the destruction of the world was apparently only the first part of the turning of the kalpa. Some of the chapters made references to the afterlife, describing the serpentine queues that would stretch through the many halls of King Yama's palace. There, sinners would have to wait for their turn to be brought to King Yama for the review of their life records and the determination of their sentences.

The sentences meted out by King Yama would invariably send non-believers to one of Di Yu's eighteen levels, where they will be punished according to the specialty of each hell. Because of the sheer number of cases, both the cold and hot hells will be full of the condemned, keeping busy all of King Yama's demonic torturers. Each of the nine groups singled out by the Maitreya, however, would be flung into Abi City, the deepest and most horrible of Di Yu's hot hells.

Going through the book, I gradually noticed that the nine groups represented an eclectic mix of people in the Philippines. I found this odd, since this meant that the scope of the sect's beliefs on salvation and punishment was not limited to the Chinese–Filipino community. The first five groups consisted of people who have abused their power. Chapter two involved the Maitreya warning politicians against taking advantage of their positions, explicitly singling out those who dispense public funds to build patronage, while chapter three contained an attack on corrupt bureaucrats. The next two chapters then dealt with errant members of the police and media. Following the chapter on the greediness of the wealthy, however, the Maitreya's focus noticeably shifted to groups of people who have committed various sins.

After the expected warning to kidnappers and other criminals, militant activists were chastised for their disruptive behaviour and their devotion to false ideologies. In the same manner, the Catholic clergy and other religious groups were also assailed for spreading the false dharma. I barely had time to think about this rigidity, when I was stunned to read that the last ones addressed by the Maitreya were those who have betrayed their family by selfishly leaving them before the end of the kalpa.

I tried to remain as level-headed as possible as I read the chapter. While I noted that there was still nothing that explicitly linked my family to the Righteous Way of the Loyal Children of Heaven Society, I nevertheless felt that my suspicions had been confirmed.

As I may have probably told you, Miriam and I had a difficult time during our first couple of months in Vancouver as we tried to adjust to our new life without the certainty of employment or the approval of our immigration status. Although we had left Manila with the highest of expectations, the weeks of stagnation had dampened our morale, and we began to question if our decision to leave had been made rashly. During this time, the frequent calls from the family were definitely encouraging and comforting. As we gradually settled into our new environment, however, the frequency of these calls decreased and eventually stopped altogether. This bothered me, especially when my attempts to call Manila only led to coldly clipped conversations about how busy things were over there and how they would call me back.

These return calls never materialized, and the best thing I could do was to concentrate on going about with our increasingly busy life. I figured that while they were probably dealing with some issues back there, I had no real reason to worry, since they would immediately call if there was an emergency. Consequently, I did not hear from them until two years later, when Raul surprised me by calling to say that he was going to be in town for a couple of days.

Raul and I had been really close growing up. We had been born months apart and had gone to the same schools until college. This made him my regular companion, especially during the late-night drinking binges of our teens and twenties that occasionally ended in one of Manila's numerous strip joints and massage parlours, including a memorably expensive night at the Valhalla Club when it was still open. All this made Raul's phone call a pleasant surprise, and I really looked forward to waxing nostalgic with him over a couple of beers.

On his first night in town, Raul met us for dinner at Yangtze, a small Chinese restaurant that we had recommended for its food and nearness to his hotel. Despite his warm handshake and buss on Miriam's cheek, I knew that things were different as soon as we sat down. Right before we ordered, Raul informed us that he had become a vegetarian, and then declined my offer of a beer. At that moment, I knew that this was not the Raul I grew up with, who regularly boasted of having once gone through three pounds of steak, and whose first words to me when he was released by his kidnappers was that he needed a cold brew.

Although there was sense in Raul's cryptic explanation that he had changed his lifestyle before it was too late, it certainly did not help the flow of our conversation. The drunken reunion that I had expected became an awkward question-and-answer session as Raul quizzed us about our life in Canada, thrice asking if we were content and happy, while only giving general answers about the state of affairs in Manila. Looking back, I should have been more suspicious than anything else, especially when Raul told us towards the end of our dinner that he would be going back to Manila the next day, since he had already finished what he needed to do. However, I have to admit that Raul's behaviour, which I attributed then to the tendency of people to change over time, left me confused and slightly hurt, so much so that Miriam had to tell me as we talked about things on the way home that it would probably be best to focus on our new life, rather than dwell on things that we couldn't understand.

Together with the contents of that chapter and my earlier observations and recollections, these memories were difficult to accept. Everything—from the presence of the temple to Raul's odd behaviour in Vancouver, and even the caretaker's assertion that I was never mentioned in his decade of employment, seemed to make sense. I tried to think of other possibilities and explanations that could shake the absurd notion that my family was entrenched in the sect and had somewhat disowned me for emigrating right before what they thought was the end of the world. I couldn't think of any, save for the nagging questions of why Tai Ma had actually encouraged the decision for me to leave, why Raul would go through the trouble of telling me that he was going to Vancouver, and why they even bothered to call me about Tai Ma's death.

As I continued reading, even these apparent discrepancies began to make sense. I realized that Tai Ma had wanted to test my loyalty, and when that didn't work out, they actually tried to get me to repent and go back. Even though I didn't know if she had authored the book, I was certain that Tai Ma was aware of its prophecies. However, for whatever reason, I think she only began indoctrinating and mobilizing the other members of the family shortly after I left, probably because Raul's kidnapping and my departure made her sense that the end of the kalpa was drawing near. This explained the gradual change in the phone calls and the eventual construction of the temple. Additionally, I thought that Raul was instructed to go to Vancouver to find out if we were really intent on staying there. What else could have explained his persistent questions, and the surprising quickness of his visit? My undesirable response must have made an impression on them, since they did not call until they informed me about Tai Ma's death more than a decade later. If the rule on succession was followed then the leadership of the sect must have been handed down by then to Aunt Raquel, since Grand Uncle Victor was the only one of his generation who was still alive. Aunt Raquel, or whoever inherited the title of Grand Matriarch of the Righteous Way, must have seen Tai Ma's death as an opportunity to bring me back and convert me. They probably knew that they would not be able to achieve this by excluding me or doing things that would make me suspicious so they tried to give a sense of as much normalcy as possible, treating me throughout the wake and funeral in the cordial manner that can be expected from long-separated relatives with whom nothing much can be discussed. I was sure that they wanted me to find out about things indirectly though, since they didn't really bother to conceal the evidence, and might have even planted the book in a spot where I was sure to find it.

You can probably tell that all these thoughts were as confusing as they were exhausting. While I certainly didn't discount the possibility that the sequence of events did not play out according to the situation I had just described, I was too engrossed to dwell on this. Not that it would've mattered, since I was certain that some form of betrayal and deception had gone into play.

As I finished reading the last portion of the chapter, however, it suddenly occurred to me that I had, in a way, also betrayed them by choosing to leave during a very difficult time. Moreover, if they had really believed in the teachings of the sect, didn't their attempts to bring me back indicate that they cared enough to try and save me from what they thought was eternal damnation? The sudden impact of these realizations blurred my surroundings, and as I struggled to flip through the remaining pages, I realized that I wasn't even sure if I was hurt, angry, or ashamed, or if any of these were even justifiable.

The last few chapters of the book contained an assortment of technical information as charts and diagrams illustrated the secret knowledge of the Righteous Way of the Loyal Children of Heaven Society. A chapter on cultivating the body through martial arts contained numerous drawings that showed different stances and movements. This was followed by a diverse collection of information on healing, which ranged from the massage of several vital points in the body, to a number of spells written on charms that had to be burned and ingested. A list of chants then accompanied a chapter on meditation, which was followed by several vegetarian recipes. Finally, the last chapter dealt with divination and the use of magic, which mainly revolved around the transfer of chi among beings.

Although these last few chapters would have normally been of great interest, I could only read them mechanically. I was still distracted by everything, and to see technical descriptions of burned medicinal charms and the transfer of chi to inanimate objects only served to loosen my concentration even more. For some strange reason, I knew that I had to revisit that chapter, and was actually quite relieved when I finished reading the book's last few characters.

While it would have been easy enough to pilfer the book, I somehow felt that I had no claim over it. Additionally, in spite of my emotional state, I was aware that quite some time had passed since I arrived, and that I still hadn't started looking for the documents I needed. This compelled me to immediately start copying the chapter into my notebook. Although my translation of the verse sections may not be poetic, I think that I have captured the meaning of what I managed to copy, which I have reproduced below.

Chapter Ten: Those Who Have Abandoned Their Family

The Ancient Buddha Maitreya opened up the Book of Heaven and took a clear look at all the countries under heaven where those who have selfishly abandoned their family reside without shame. Living in secure apartments and houses with gardens and pools, deceiving themselves by being relieved at having escaped the darkness and gunfire amid the loosening of the earth and the storm of flames, they work without remembering the four sources of gratitude. Drinking wine and eating meat, disloyal to their ancestors, they reject the Righteous Way.

Among them are those unthinking ones who, upon the first sign of trouble, immediately leave with their wife, son, and daughter, going far away, disguising their fear and ambition as opportunity. Relying on these, they work hard and are deaf to the call of the village; however, since their deeds are distanced from the good of their elders, brothers, and sisters, none of their cowardly efforts have merit and only add to their offences.

Therefore, during the transformative cataclysm, this type of person will be taken back to hell, never to rise again. If, however, you are willing to clear your heart and see that you want to return then repent and begin to obey the Righteous Way. Become vegetarian, don't do evil deeds, and strengthen your mind and body through meditation and exercise. Once you have repented then all your transgressions will be forgiven.

The Ancient Buddha looked and saw those who have left.
Hiding as if heaven and earth are blind to their sins.

In the years of the true dharma all cultivated their karma.
In the years of the false dharma virtue has all but disappeared.

Twelve thousand years ago we practised the Way as one family.
And now you've cast off the energy of your previous lives.

Because of blind ambition and cowardice, you've forgotten your home.
Your journeys to the east and the west have confused you.

Now you are lost and have no memory of your ancestors.
You'll regret this later, when the future kalpa arrives.

When the land is barren and the world is in turmoil, you'll return to Di Yu.
King Yama will be displeased and will judge harshly.

Oxhead and Horse Face will throw you nine hundred thousand *li* into Abi City.
Your soul will forever be tossed among the eighty-one-thousand sufferings.

I urge you to cleanse from your heart the mundane world, return, repent.
Avoid eternity in Abi City and disgrace to your family.

Uphold vegetarianism, respect your parents, and walk the Righteous Way.
Live according to the true dharma and King Yama will send you back to Cloud City.

The August Buddha, the great turner of the Dharma Wheel, looked at those who have brought tears to the Eternal Venerable Mother's eyes. On the third day of the third month of the *chia-tzu* year, where will . . .

As you can see, I was unable to copy the chapter in its entirety. The first few paragraphs were difficult to transcribe. My hand kept on trembling as I wrote, perhaps because of all the confusion, or maybe because it was hard to write Chinese characters for the first time since high school. By the bottom portion of the third paragraph, though, I was working at a steady pace, and even felt that I could finish the task soon enough.

Just as I was beginning to get comfortable and my confidence was starting to pick up, something happened that was so strange, confusing, and terrifying that I still continue to think about it. As I was starting to copy the first part of the verse section, I noticed that the characters seemed to be fading away. At first, I thought that my eyes were just getting tired from all the reading or that I had lost track of time so much that night had fallen, and I had forgotten to switch on the lights. However, it soon became clear that the characters were really disappearing. Although I was naturally shocked, I quickly recovered to resume copying as fast as I could. I guess my desire to copy that chapter was just greater than anything else at the time.

Despite my frenetic pace, I only managed to get to where my translation ended. By then, all the characters in the book had disappeared. Even the title and the illustration on the cover page were gone. As I flipped through the empty pages of the crumbling volume though, it occurred to me that it was probably good that I wasn't able to complete copying that whole chapter. Otherwise, what I copied might have disappeared as well. I must have contemplated this for quite some time, since I felt exhausted when I finally stood up. I understood that it was useless for me to look for all those documents and that I had to leave the compound immediately. Just like I was certain that I would be spending the rest of my days waiting and that I would religiously and without merit whisper the Wordless True Sutra during the times when I was sure that I was alone, I knew that I would never be going back. There was nothing else for me in Manila, and my only consolation was the knowledge that I would be going home in a couple of days.

The Lament of Philip Reyes

Philip Reyes had no regrets that you'll never read this. It allowed him to be honest about things that can destroy what's left of his reputation. Philip had been having a bad day. The insurance adjuster had called that morning to ask for copies of the receipts for the hundreds of eyeglass frames and all the equipment destroyed during the fire. When Philip asked why he didn't bring this up during their initial meeting a few months ago as well as in his numerous follow up calls, the adjuster merely replied that what he needed would form the basis for depreciated value.

This additional delay was disheartening. The past months had steadily depleted his meagre savings, not to mention added to the abuse and accusations heaped on him by his creditors. Consequently, as he was driving home a few hours later, he received another call, this time from William Tan, once a close friend from elementary who had lent him money to fast-track his purchase of a specular microscope.

While Philip had already repaid ₱600,000 out of the ₱700,000 he owed, he struggled to make good on the balance after the fire. William steadily became more condescending and hostile as the months passed, leading to this phone call to tell him that his cheque for the remainder of the balance and interest had bounced.

Philip had actually tried texting and calling him several times over the past weeks, asking him to defer the deposit of that cheque, which he would replace before it became stale. Save for a supposedly missent text saying that the cheque had already been deposited and nothing could prepare that broke piece-of-shit for what he was planning, Philip never received a reply.

After calling him a swindler and a thief, William said that Philip had picked the wrong person to cheat and that he had heard from reliable sources that he had reopened his clinic. Philip tried explaining that he had used most of his savings to set up that small clinic, which had none of the equipment that he needed to survive, let alone pay creditors.

William only repeated that Philip didn't know who he was messing with, and before hanging up, told him that he was a small-time doctor who expected him to be impressed by a ₱200,000 monthly income, when he could easily laugh off millions in a typical trading day.

As if Philip's day couldn't get worse, the typhoon that was expected to spare Metro Manila had changed course, bringing a steadily increasing downpour that eventually obstructed all views of the road. Over the radio, it became apparent that the floodwaters were approaching unprecedented levels, with roads and even entire subdivisions getting submerged as people looked for higher ground while helplessly witnessing their homes, neighbours, and loved ones disappear in the flood. Philip tried to focus on the road while trying to reassure himself that his uninsured clinic was on the third floor of a building in a somewhat elevated area.

Since he knew that all possible routes were through flooded areas, Philip decided to take a short detour, turning right at Lazaro de Chino to seek shelter at the casino of the Royal Crown of Manila Hotel.

Although Philip hadn't been back since the fire, and his gambling had always been low stakes, he would occasionally win big at the Royal's casino during some particularly bad days, such as the preventable blinding of long-time patients or when a malfunctioning slit lamp led him to refer patients to other clinics. It probably also helped that his father used to bring him to the Royal when he was a child, decades before the casino opened.

Back then, the Royal was one of Manila's finest hotels, where the country's socialites, politicians, and businessmen would gather. While its lobby lounge popularized high tea in fashionable circles, its continental restaurant gained fame for the calibre of its French chef.

Sadly, time had been harsh to the Royal, with its famed outlets long replaced by rows of concessionaires peddling shoddy knockoffs, while the musty, faded carpeting did little to hide the chips and nicks all over the marble floors. Aside from the rumours of its owners owing close to a billion pesos in back taxes, perhaps the most telltale sign of the Royal's decline was the conversion of its entire sixth floor into a massage parlour.

All this was far from Philip's mind as he made his way up from the basement parking, past the faded photographs framed along the cramped stairwell. He could still hear the downpour as he approached the casino entrance at the opposite end of the lobby, where the guards distractedly checked his bag while listening intently to the news.

Inside, the rain was masked by indistinct muzak occasionally interrupted by high-pitched rings from the slot machines clustered near the entrance. It was cold, and there were hardly any people, which was expected because of the weather and the fact that the Royal could not compete with the sprawling, foreign-backed casinos that had recently opened nearby.

Philip walked towards the ATM. It was tough for him to see ₱10,000 left in his savings account, especially with the expected closure of his checking account by William's deposit. He decided to withdraw ₱5,000. It may have been reckless to withdraw half of his available cash as his casino bankroll, but the amount was really too insignificant. Besides, all this didn't factor in the possibility of him winning.

Philip went to the tables, ignoring the empty stares of the bored baccarat and blackjack dealers to sit at the casino's lone Caribbean stud poker table, where he converted his money into chips.

Despite its reputation for having bad odds and none of the skilled aspects of real poker, Caribbean stud had always appealed to Philip. Although he once tried to impress a hot dealer by saying that the heart of the game was the over nineteen trillion possible combinations in a fifty-two-card deck, the truth was decidedly less profound. It had more to do with the steady pace of each round and the relative absence of self-blame when playing according to the general rule of raising only with the dealer's qualifying hand or higher.

Looking up, Philip saw that the progressive jackpot had only increased by a couple of thousand since his last visit.

He mentioned this to the dealer as he placed the minimum bet of 300. The dealer chuckled and told Philip that he should just get the jackpot, since it had been there for so long.

While the prospect of winning over a million pesos in one deal made Philip think of being able to fix his life without needing to wait, he knew that receiving a royal flush was extremely unlikely. Instead, he should have tempered his hopes to being distracted throughout the storm while still going home with enough for gas and food.

However, even these modest goals seemed distant as the game started with Philip folding thrice, making him consider having to spend the night in his car or the equally depressing hotel lobby. Thankfully, Philip got three kings on his next deal, and was relieved that the dealer qualified with a pair of deuces.

That hand was pivotal as Philip started to win, his hands with multipliers always managing to qualify. With Philip's two pairs, trips, and the occasional straight leading to double, triple, or even quadruple his raise, he was soon increasing bets, bringing his stack of chips to around ₱40,000 after thirty minutes.

Despite his luck, Philip found it hard to concentrate. Any enjoyment from his growing stack was taken away by the awareness of how distant this was from what he needed. Mercifully, he saw that the casino sold brandy by the bottle, which he promptly bought with a few chips.

The cold encouraged Philip to drink the brandy neat. He hadn't had that particular brand since his internship days, so his first sips were rough. Gradually, though, the liquor mellowed, enabling him to refill the snifter with increasing frequency. It soon served its purpose as Philip began to immerse himself in the game, even adding a layer of suspense by revealing his hands through identifying the cards by their pips.

Philip had already reduced the bottle to a quarter when he realized that he had been dealt eights over fours. He was betting 2,500 as his ante by then, so he hurriedly raised 5,000.

His full house qualified with the dealer's trio of sixes, bringing him seven times his raise, the corresponding jackpot prize of 5,000, and his ante. For the first time in months, he was ecstatic. After tipping the dealer, Philip beamed with the confidence that the world was his.

The cigarette girl passed by as Philip was fixing his chips. Her presence made him aware that he had not been with a woman in almost a year. Although he found her plain, Philip whistled her over to ask when her shift would end while attempting to grope what he could. Despite the cigarette girl's initial embarrassment and polite refusals, she eventually jerked away, flatly telling Philip that he was too old and ugly for her.

Philip tried to mask his wounded pride by turning his back on the cigarette girl to tell the dealer to resume their game. Although Philip won the next deals, he felt ill at ease. Somehow, experience led him to believe that it was only a matter of time before he had to leave the table or risk losing everything. By the time he had lost five straight deals, Philip knew that he had to go, so, after downing the rest of the brandy, he hurriedly stood up with his chips, trying his best to avoid eye contact with the cigarette girl.

Philip cashed out a little over ₱100,000. Admittedly, it occurred to him to play another table game or try the slots. However, he decided that it would be best to just get a room. A lot had happened over the course of the day, and Philip was drunk and exhausted, to the point that he only realized that he was no longer in the casino when he noticed the sound of the downpour, and the clerk behind the reception desk asked if he could be of any assistance.

Philip asked the clerk for the room rates. Although the hourly rates were appealing, he decided to settle for the cheapest overnight room. After getting his deposit and giving Philip some forms to sign, the clerk mechanically opened a drawer to retrieve a key fastened to a huge wooden keychain. He handed this to Philip then pointed to his left, saying that the elevators were behind the column near the bathroom, and if he had to leave the hotel premises, he would have to return the key for safekeeping.

Pressing the black elevator button, Philip could do little else but drowsily stare as the lights on the overhead board counted down the floor numbers. Stepping inside, he noticed that the elevator was silent and, with the exception of a yellowed mayor's permit and a discoloured flyer for a promo from six years ago, bare. For a few moments, he wasn't sure if the elevator was working, since the inverted button to the fourth floor failed to light up. Thankfully, the doors closed, and the elevator slowly crawled up to what would be his home for the next few hours.

It was immediately clear as the elevator doors opened that the guest areas had also been neglected. The presence of several busted lights did little to hide the dirty floral carpets that had probably been there since the 1970s.

The room was by no means welcoming. The bathroom was covered in yellow mosaic tiles, with a bar of soap, a sachet of shampoo, and a toothbrush set placed on a towel that was draped on the side of the bathtub. The room itself was humid, and while Philip was concerned about mould, he was tired and dizzy. He decided to take off his clothes, piling them on one of the single beds before pulling off the blue and pink quilt from the other to slip under the sheets, ignoring the novelty of the old, box-type television while he tried to sleep.

As tired and drunk as he was, Philip was restless. He felt flushed and the sound of the rain provided an incessant reminder of the day's events. More worryingly, despite his other problems, he kept on revisiting his encounter with the cigarette girl.

Even if he had been rejected in worse ways and could barely remember her beyond a vague uniform, Philip kept thinking about the girl. He tried several times to recreate that unfortunate interaction. Vague bits and pieces, such as a futile reconstruction of the feel of her flesh, and the possible shapes of her breasts, frustrated and upset him, adding to the discomfort brought about by the room's humidity. All this made him itch, and he began to scratch different parts of his body until they bled.

While all this made Philip realize that he would probably be unable to sleep, it also made him think about something that he had always overlooked. In a way, his professional life had been based on similarities in human physiology and the prescription of remedies culled from precedents. Since human anatomy could be viewed collectively and generally, it was only misplaced sentimentality caused by wounded pride that made him dwell on that cigarette girl, who would be indistinguishable from the collective magnitude of humanity. This realization was enough for Philip to get dressed and proceed to the sixth floor.

Although he had never been inside since it opened, the Valkyrie Spa at the Royal had earned a reputation as a popular massage parlour. Despite its apparent allusions to an infamous, prohibitively expensive nightclub that abruptly closed when Philip was still an undergrad, there was no definite link between the two.

Instead of the drab, faded neglect that permeated throughout the hotel, the Valkyrie Spa's lobby had been modelled with mirrored walls and floors of black and white marble slabs. Although he was certain that the storm was still raging outside, Philip could not hear the rain. All this brought about an atmosphere similar to that of a high-end lounge, which was somehow broken by the dimmed blue lights and the price list of services posted right behind the receptionist, who, upon seeing Philip, asked how she could help.

Philip replied that he wanted to see the aquarium. A uniformed attendant emerged to bring him to the viewing area, which was a one-way glass pane that separated customers from the girls who were seated on two couches behind the glass.

There were only two girls—one on each couch, both not wearing any uniform, although they did have numbers pinned to their chests. While number 87, who was in a tight white shirt and short shorts, appeared fixated on her phone; 196, wearing jeans and a blouse, was watching television.

Philip must've stood there awhile as the attendant apologetically said that most of the other girls had not been able to report because of the weather. It had been a slow night, and the therapists were just waiting for the storm to end so that they could go home. Either of them, though, were available, and both had always received good feedback from guests.

Philip asked the attendant if it would be possible to get them both. The attendant replied that a twin massage could be arranged but would mean payment for two rooms plus the extra service. Philip nodded and was led back to the reception area, where he paid the receptionist ₱3,000, not even bothering to question why she said his massage would last for the standard ninety minutes when he had paid for the equivalent of two sessions. With everything he drank leaving him disoriented, acidic, and dehydrated, he knew that he wouldn't last long.

After declining the receptionist's offer for an official receipt, Philip was led by the attendant to the room, which, although similar to the hotel room, had been extensively renovated, with a steam-equipped shower and a flat-screen television, in addition to several mirrors on the ceiling.

The attendant left as soon as Philip entered. He must've fallen asleep since he woke up to a throbbing head and knocking on the door. 87 and 196 entered and introduced themselves with obvious stage names. As Philip shook their hands, he told them his name was Junjun. This led one girl to flash a brace-filled smile, telling him he was lucky that both Junjuns will be given special attention by two beautiful women. Not knowing how to respond, Philip kept silent until the other girl pointed out that he reeked of alcohol, and that he should at least brush his teeth.

The girls started to strip while Philip brushed. From where he stood, he could see in the mirror that one had full breasts, untrimmed pubic hair, and a prominent c-section scar that was as dark as her areola. This served as a contrast to the pinkish nipples of the other girl's slightly sagging breasts and clean-shaven crotch. As one of them went into the shower to temper the water's temperature, the other made some adjustments to the control panel for the steam. Once satisfied, they told Philip to join them.

It was hard for Philip to see inside the shower. As the girls moved their hands around his body and he felt the contours and creases on theirs, he realized that his penis was numb, and more troublingly, limp.

After patting him dry, the girls led Philip to the bed, where one straddled his back and began to massage his shoulders, while the other worked on his legs. Although it felt good to be touched by two pairs of hands, the knots on his back remained largely untouched, leaving Philip somewhat disappointed when he was told to turn over and asked if he wanted extra service.

Philip nodded, leading one of the girls to reach into her purse for a condom. She then started to lick his glans while playing with his scrotum as the other girl teased his nipples with her tongue and lips, softly brushing her drooping breasts against his stomach.

Despite these efforts, Philip was unable to muster an erection. After what seemed like an eternity, the girls changed their approach, with one rubbing her groin against his shaft, while the other concentrated on his erogenous zones. When this failed, they shifted to a more direct method, taking turns at grabbing and jerking his penis rapidly.

This led to an unbearable pain that made Philip ask for a break. Knowing better, the girls said that it would be better if he just rest, with one of them mock-scolding him for having arrived drunk. Although Philip closed his eyes, he was unable to sleep, becoming, instead, a passive eavesdropper to the girls' conversation as they went through topics that ranged from their daily commutes, how unlucky it was for them to report on the day of the storm, to parenting tips, and the cover stories that they told their husbands. This went on until there was a knock on the door, and the attendant said that their time was up. The girls then told Philip to wake up, and after handing each ₱1,500, he went back to his room, deflated and angry.

As Philip lay on the bed and heard nothing else but the rain, he kept on thinking of ways to redeem himself. He had wasted money in trying to prove a point and had failed to the point that his virility had been put into question. The least he could do was to effect and maintain an erection until climax. Discounting an immediate return to the Valkyrie Spa, he decided that his best option was to accomplish this himself.

There were only two adult options on the old television—an American and a Japanese one, both productions from the early 1990s that seemed to have been lifted from VHS tapes that had either been frequently used or copied numerous times. Philip settled on the American film, starting with soft strokes while watching a blonde writhe in ecstasy, her garbled moans breaking the storm's monotony.

While all this was more comforting than arousing, he began to make a conscious effort to imagine himself as the blonde's partner. As Philip synchronized his pulls, he grew aware that his efforts weren't working. He knew that there was a psychological factor in getting an erection, so he persisted, to the point that his wrists were beginning to tire when a sudden power surge caused the lights to flicker and the television screen to reset to static.

Despite the remote's presence at Philip's side, he made no move to reach for it. Instead, he continued to stare blankly at the screen, mindlessly looking at the black and white patterns of the static's noise, too exhausted and defeated on so many levels that he wasn't able to immediately react when everything began.

In fairness to Philip, there might not have been enough time to react. He suspected that everything may have only lasted for less than a second since it took a while for the reset clock to progress to 12.01 once it was over. Philip also knew that what he witnessed was something that could not accurately be captured in words. Nonetheless, he believed that he owed it to you to recount the experience, even if he were only capable of covering a miniscule speck distorted by linear progression.

As Philip stared at the screen, the movement of the black and white particles began to accelerate, coalescing and separating in various patterns until there was a sudden ripple that caused everything to break into fragments and reassemble into an infinite multitude of video-like scenarios featuring the delivery of the same newborn baby, whose multiplied cries, along with the background murmur of different voices, seemed to drown out the storm.

Philip did not immediately recognize the baby as himself until he saw that it was his own mother who had given birth and remembered that he had looked that way in an old photograph. Having last seen his mother during her funeral years ago, it was unnerving for Philip to see her in her youth, her face exhausted from labour, multiplied in never-ending visions, each one distinct from the other in some way.

Philip saw his mother give birth to him in different places—in cars, in the middle of random streets, in the ubiquitous movie theatres and shopping arcades of the time, in a wide array of houses and apartments, and in different hospitals. While he understandably failed to recognize the hospitals, Philip somehow knew that one of them had to be the actual place where he was born, although it wouldn't have mattered. Though the delivery rooms may have been identical in some, there were varied configurations for each, with different doctors performing the c-section, deciding or foregoing an episiotomy, various nurses, and the occasional presence of his weary father, who had also been dead for decades.

Even when the people involved happened to be the same, there were differences in what transpired. These differences ranged from something as innocuous as the presence of an engagement ring or a crucifix on a nurse, or a change in the unintelligible dialogue as doctors and nurses coordinated with one another. There was an instance in which, to Philip's horror, a nurse accidentally dropped him. This led that particular scene to divide, with one showing the newborn Philip in a slowly growing pool of blood fading and disappearing, while several variations appeared of the confused panic on the faces of everyone as they tried to resuscitate him.

Although seeing himself die soon after being born was disturbing, it was impossible for Philip to dwell on it. The scene's disappearance, along with the immediate appearance of multiple aftermaths in which he had survived, didn't allow him to mourn for himself. Somehow, Philip knew that his presence was enough reassurance that this was not how things had happened. This allowed him to settle into a resigned acceptance as he saw similarly fatal accidents in different configurations in various places, as well as more gruesome ones, such as a midwife accidentally hitting his head on the corner of a table, and his mother strangling him in a delirious frenzy.

Philip saw variations of his mother dying from the trauma of labour, of his father suffering strokes in his waiting anxiety, and of him being accidentally switched at birth. Together with other unlikely scenarios, these gave rise to homecomings that ensured a childhood far removed from what he had experienced. Aside from his childhood house, Philip saw himself being brought home to unfamiliar mansions, apartments, and shanties in various parts of Manila, in different provinces, in other countries. He saw himself being nurtured by his mother, alone, or with domestic help; breastfed, or forced to take nourishment from sporadic doses of formula.

Death followed Philip in all these homecomings. Whether it was him being smothered by a mentally ill *yaya* to dampen his cries as he lay in an ornate crib or his final death rattle as he wasted away from malnutrition in a makeshift shack, the visions always ended by fading into darkness before being replaced by alternative scenarios in which he had survived.

Except for the times when the brush with death left a physical scar or infirmity, these escapes went mostly blissfully unnoticed. As these misses multiplied, Philip saw himself move from infancy into childhood. As often as he saw himself die from disease or violence, so did he see himself subject to circumstances beyond his control.

Philip saw his life change as his parents made, maintained, and squandered fortunes. From anchoring his existence in a small locality that determined all aspects of his life to being perpetually on the move, he saw himself submerged in the mundane aspects of his existence as he lived, survived, and died.

By the time Philip reached what would have been his third birthday, he found it impossible to keep track of the torrent of faces, places, and conversations that seemed to converge into an incoherent mess. He was just about to give up when he saw variations of himself at the beach, posing with his father as his mother took photographs. He immediately recognized these scenes from a sepia picture that he had found and kept from his mother's personal effects that was captioned as Philip's first visit to the beach at Puerto Azul.

This allowed Philip to refocus his attention on a vaguely recognizable childhood that brought back and animated fragments of memory, often in ways that had not been possible. Whether he was surrounded by siblings, including a sister who he knew was the miscarriage that he had heard about from his parents during unguarded moments, or he was subject to the practical jokes of an uncle who had died years before he had been born, Philip chose to see himself grow up in an environment not far removed from the relative privilege of his youth.

Consequently, Philip saw himself almost always accompanied by a uniform-clad yaya on his first day of school, which he usually survived. School allowed him to meet other children, creating an interchangeable pool of peers that led to friends, acquaintances, and rivals.

It was odd for Philip to recognize some of his classmates, especially those he barely remembered as children, and some who he had forgotten until that moment. These included the chalk-eating classmate whose family ran several low-end funeral parlours, as well as the braggart son of big-time smugglers who eventually had to transfer to a cheaper school once his family's connections were no longer in power. He also saw some classmates who had never gone to his school but were instantly recognizable. Among them were the child actor whose fans would wait outside the gates at every dismissal and the son of the country's richest man, whose bodyguards were given special permission to stay on campus—something taken to another level by the president's own son, who had members of the constabulary stationed near the classrooms throughout the day.

With the exception of the times he died, became disabled, or witnessed his family go through difficulties that forced him to stop his education, school played direct and tangential roles in developing Philip's hobbies, phobias, and prejudices, which evolved according to the different experiences he went through in classroom activities and summer vacations.

This meant that Philip saw himself taking up a variety of hobbies and interests, which brought about variable evolutions based on sequences of events. Whether swimming led to water polo, or a library book borrowed by accident sparked zeal for an obscure topic, he saw himself grow up, evolving in interconnected ways that were occasionally terminated prematurely.

Philip saw himself age as his personality and interests evolved. With birthdays and milestones, he eventually hit puberty. Philip saw himself develop an awareness of the opposite sex as his body matured. This awareness was kindled in different ways, which ranged from his finding illustrations in a book on reproductive health or discovering his father's stash of pornographic magazines, to getting a first erection while being bathed by a yaya, who, in some instances, introduced Philip to the pleasures of the female body.

Although Philip saw himself father a child in a few variants of that introduction, the implications did not really occur to him since he was distracted by the notion that any girl could have been his. He let his concentration falter and allowed himself to veer away from the relatively familiar, once again taking in images from lives that he could neither place nor contextualize.

Philip saw himself become intimate with women of various ages and persuasions. Aside from prostitutes and girls his age, there were starlets, lady guards, sales ladies, tourists, market vendors, golf caddies, factory workers, socialites, and even nuns. While there was an undeniable excitement in seeing the variety of women that he could have experienced in his youth, Philip found it impossible to follow the succession of faces and bodies as he saw himself go through life as a young adult, with sex being a miniscule factor in the jumbled mess of branching sequences that offered no opportunity to distinguish between love and heartbreak, triumph and loss.

Since the only respite were the blank visions of death that incessantly branched into the multitudes and variants of situations where he survived, Philip began to get nauseated. This nausea got to the point that he was already retching when he saw her among a group of nursing students undergoing their practicum orientation at a circular workstation while a version of himself as an intern nonchalantly worked on a typewriter.

While she was never assigned to the ward where he worked, seeing this somewhat familiar scene brought Philip back, as he surprised himself with how he could focus and slow down specific variants of scenarios while isolating bits of conversation. This had little to do with residual nostalgia for your mother, however. Rather, it was in the knowledge that there was a possibility that some combination of events would eventually lead to you.

True enough, Philip saw a number of interactions with your mother that developed into relationships that approximated his memory. Some even involved variants of that post-duty drinking session where they actually met. This was organized by a colleague who had his eyes set on some of the nursing students, and while Philip had spent most of the night conversing with your mother, it was hard not to notice alternatives such as seeing a very drunk version of himself vomit on her in an unsuccessful attempt to make it to the bathroom.

As Philip saw parallel relationships with your mother, it was hard for him not to notice how young they were. Despite being adults at the time, the relationships that Philip saw were characterized by cryptic pager messages, impromptu sing-alongs to the radio, and trysts in dimly lit public places. This allowed him to recall what had happened as he saw versions of the day that she first told him about you.

He was in Hong Kong for a conference at the time and had received an envelope containing a fax message.

Whether the message was written in her characteristically large handwriting or typewritten or if he read it on the way to the venue or during a session break, it conveyed the urgent need to contact her. Since she had done similar things during his previous trips, Philip had actually expected her to say that her emergency was that she missed him. Instead, as he saw himself using different payphones at the Admiralty MTR station, Philip knew that she was telling him that she was pregnant.

Seeing himself approach the platform after each call had ended, Philip remembered thinking that he had no way to atone for what he had done. Although he saw himself give in to these warped notions in some instances and jump in front of the approaching train and almost always into the darkness of that scenario's end, Philip remembered regaining his composure with the thought that more than anything, important decisions would have to be made upon his return to Manila.

Philip then focused on scenarios that made him recall his first weeks back. From that initial embrace when she fetched him from the airport, they never got a chance to decide. There were days when she would tell him that he would make a good father, and that for whatever reason, she was certain that you were going to be a boy. They would then browse stores for cribs and strollers while they discussed the future. On other days, she would talk about getting an abortion, to which Philip would always tell her that this would ultimately be her choice. She probably knew that this hurt him, though, since she would repeatedly punch her abdomen during arguments, even when these concerned the preparations for their would-be family.

Remembering that period was difficult for Philip, who had never really forgiven himself for asking to see a single test result or for not conferring with her gynaecologist, who was actually a mentor in medical school. This oversight finally came to a head in the middle of the third week, when she told him that there had been a mistake. This led to a short period of frequent, intense quarrelling followed by a gradual drifting apart that culminated in her leaving him for good.

As Philip saw instances that had him review test results or place a phone call, the only sequences that held his interest were those that would have led to your birth. This had him paying little attention to your mother's different pregnancy cravings, the situations that had them married, and even the times she miscarried, as he anticipated your delivery. These scenes came soon enough, and he saw you born in various locations and circumstances, with some even taking place in what seemed to be similar, if not the same, delivery rooms to his own birth.

He assisted with your birth in several scenarios. He saw some where you were stillborn. Seeing himself in the aftermath of holding your lifeless, misshapen body was surprising for Philip, as he never knew that he was capable of feeling such pain. This became more palpable in the scenes where you died shortly after being born, and in the variations of your wake and funeral that had them attend to guests in the presence of your tiny coffin.

Aside from the ever-present possibilities of loss and grief, Philip also saw whimsical domestic moments. For every time he saw you die in an accident or from an undetected congenital condition, there were scenes that were as innocuous as their attempts to get you to remain still for a first family portrait, or the inopportune instances that you needed food or a diaper change.

Philip saw that settling into a domesticated life gradually involved taking on increasing amounts of responsibility to create a home that would set the foundations for your future. While this meant that he saw regret and self-blame in the aftermath of situations where you were involved in an otherwise avoidable mishap or where you were somehow lost or kidnapped, it also meant that he and your mother were so engrossed in the various configurations of their day-to-day activities that your birthday parties and the periodic need to buy new clothes became fleeting reminders of your rapid growth that, for whatever reason, was barely noticed in the recurring scenes of your watching cartoons on VHS during weekends.

He saw you enter pre-school, then elementary. Nowhere else did fatherly responsibility become apparent to Philip as when he dealt with your school. Of course, these would have been similar to meeting the relatives of patients, but as he saw himself occasionally confide in your mother that it was hard not to see these parent–teacher conferences as a sign that you were beginning to develop a life external to them and that you were on your way to becoming your own person.

Before long, Philip saw himself being called to your school for reasons that would have never been captured in your report card. Whether you had been bullied, were the bully, made your teacher cry, or had somehow caused a deadly accident, Philip saw that these incidents often left him aware of his inability to protect you from harm or from doing harm. Conversely, it was also not difficult for Philip to see how proud of you he was during your extracurricular events, whether you failed to play as your team lost a big basketball game, received an extra round of applause during a school play, or placed in the national math Olympiad.

While Philip also saw scenarios that left him disappointed, such as those that had you make him a young grandfather, pretty soon he began seeing scenes of your elementary graduation. Among the different variants of the festivities, one stream caught Philip's eye as it involved William Tan.

Although Philip had seen him multiple times due to their shared school experiences and the fact that William had a son who would have been your age, these scenes started with William asking about their plans for after the programme. Philip replied that the family was going to celebrate at the Royal's continental restaurant, to which William said that they would be joining them.

This led William, his wife, three children, and his mother joining you for your graduation dinner, where he told them not to be shy and to order whatever they wanted. Amid multiple orders of foie gras, prime rib, and lobster that William asked to have wrapped at the end of the night, he gleefully talked about which of their former classmates had gone broke, had marriage problems, and had earned their fortunes. Starting from William's arrival and throughout the versions of his anecdotes, Philip saw your mother maintain a forced smile as she pinched his leg from under the table. Her pinching only intensified towards the end of the night, when William brought out a folded newspaper clipping from the graduation programme and said that he read that there were plans to resurrect mammoths, and that he couldn't wait for this to happen so that he could commission artists to carve ivory pieces.

The next scenes Philip saw had him and your mother arguing after you had gone to bed. These generally began with her being upset at the bill while voicing her intense dislike for his friend. Although Philip tried to defend William by saying that he was like a brother, this only made your mother angrier, as she said that William was only his friend because of his apparent success and would hardly recognize him if his fortunes changed.

Despite everything that happened between Philip and your mother, he could never deny her excellent judgement of character. Getting his bearings back, however, he saw that he had lost you in the mix of unfamiliar scenes, faces, and locations. In this frenetic jumble of images and sounds, Philip somehow managed to see himself on the phone in his empty clinic. He immediately recognized this as his call with the insurance adjuster from earlier that day.

As Philip saw variations of that day, including some in which the typhoon had spared Manila and he had some patients come in, he saw himself leave the clinic. In some versions of this, he saw himself receive a text message from William saying that hiding from him was pointless, and that he was right behind him waiting for his payment with interest. True enough, these scenes had William's black BMW behind Philip's car.

Although he sometimes took a less confrontational option and made several detours, Philip saw scenes in which he went down in the downpour to apologize. These generally elicited hostile mocking from William, who grinned in triumph as he misapplied platitudes while telling Philip that he now knew a lot about him from his sources, to which Philip answered that he could have confronted him to ask if any of these were true.

In some scenes, William went down to shove Philip. While this triggered a fight where Philip saw himself sometimes win, lose, or get shot, he found himself drawn to sequences that had him dig his fingers into William's eyes as they struggled, and oblivious to his screams, extract both eyeballs. With the exception of a variant that had Philip spit into one of William's bloody orbits as he told him that he only needed his mouth and ears, this mostly led to his being subdued while still clenching William's eyes.

Despite the base sense of satisfaction that this sequence brought about, it was impossible to deny Philip's unease with these scenes. Although he had seen innumerable acts that left little doubt about his potential capacity for violence, what he had witnessed went against the core principles of his identity on so many different levels. This left Philip deflated to the point that he lost interest in seeing what would have happened if he had been dealt a royal flush at the Caribbean stud poker table, or if the cigarette girl had somehow reciprocated his advances.

As Philip vacantly stared into this void of possibilities, he noticed an increasing number of scenes ending in darkness. Taking a closer look, he saw that most of these involved his suicide. However, the scenes in which he saw himself slit his wrists, jump out of windows, or overdose on morphine gradually gave way to sequences that had Philip on his hotel bed, furiously, impotently, desperately jerking his limp penis while watching either of the adult films.

While these images multiplied to reach the limits of his vision and Philip felt himself fumbling for the remote, he found you again, this time at a family lunch. Aside from your mother, this scenario had both his parents alive as they watched you announce that you had been accepted with a full scholarship to the state university's accelerated medical school programme. As Philip saw the pride in the face of those present, both living and dead, he pressed the power button, aware that only the darkness of his room faintly illuminated by the alarm clock and the sound of the rain would be left. He guessed that if this would be the last time he would get to see you, it would best be on this note. Besides, deep down, Philip knew that you never really existed, anyway.

Acknowledgements

Most of these stories were written throughout the 2000s, with earlier versions first appearing in *Heights, Story Philippines,* the *Philippines Free Press, Likhaan: The Journal of Contemporary Philippine Literature,* the *Philippines Graphic,* as well as the anthologies *Philippine Speculative Fiction Volume 1, A Different Voice: Fiction by Young Filipino Writers,* and *Lauriat: A Filipino-Chinese Speculative Fiction Anthology.* Earlier versions of two stories also appeared in *Enough About Human Rights,* the fourth title in an Ateneo Institute of Literary Arts and Practices (AILAP) chapbook series that saw a limited release in 2017. Some of these stories also went through stops along the circuit of writers workshops in the Philippines, including the fourth Ateneo, forty-fifth Siliman, seventh Iyas, and fourteenth Iligan National Writers' Workshops. 'Dreaming Valhalla' won the second prize for short story in the 2007 Don Carlos Palanca Memorial Awards for Literature, while 'A Visit to the Exhibition of the International Committee on Children's Rights' won the third prize for short story in the 2007 Philippines Free Press Literary Awards.

Aside from Nora Nazerene Abu Bakar and the rest of Penguin Random House SEA, this book would not have been possible without the input, support, and encouragement of my teachers, workshop panellists, publishers, mentors, family, and friends. Although an exhaustive list would not be possible, several names come to mind. These include: Jonathan Tupaz, Jeanne Purpura, Adrian Asis, Thess Nebres-Ladrido, Danton Remoto, Max Pulan, Jun Cruz Reyes, Gad Lim, Vicente Garcia Groyon, Susan Lara, Mike Coroza, Alvin Yapan, Daisy See, Benilda Santos, Eduardo Calasanz, DM Reyes, Larry Ypil, National Artists for Literature Edith Tiempo(†), F. Sionil Jose(†), and Gemino Abad, Cesar Ruiz Aquino, Alfred Yuson, Marjorie Evasco, Shirley Lua, Anthony Tan, Charlson Ong, Merlie Alunan, Marne Kilates, Rebecca Añonuevo, Elmer Ordoñez, Christine Godinez-Ortega, Chari Lucero, Antonio Enriquez(†), Joy Enriquez(†), Noel Pingoy, Marcel Antonio, Khavn De La Cruz, Achinette Villamor, Iwa Wilwayco, Joel Toledo, Allan Popa, Sarge Lacuesta, Arkaye Kierulf, Asterio Gutierrez, Nicolas Lacson, EJ Galang, Panch Alvarez, Waps San Diego, Mikael de Lara Co, Kristian Cordero, Pocholo Goitia, Kokoy Guevarra(†), Javie Bengzon, Denise Bengzon, John Torres, Martin Ong Yambao, Kints Kintana, Ana Escalante Neri(†), Joshua Lim So, Det Neri, Kit Kwe, Michellan Sarile-Alagao, Marguerite de Leon, Martin Villanueva, Allan Derain, Adrian de Pedro, Dean Francis Alfar, Jade Bernas, Totel de Jesus, Ceres Abanil, Mia Tijam, Alyza Taguilaso, Gromyko Semper, Camilla Pante, Paolo Panelo, Pablo Singzon, Hans Tan, Gregory How, Bon Denver Syiaco, Kenneth Reyes-Lao, Marvin Gan, Benjamin Tom Wong, Angelica Candano-Salamat, Barbie Candano,

Elizabeth Candano, Patricia Limpe, Julius Limpe(†), John Alonte, Gigi Alonte, Lilith Stangenberg, Adrien Lamande, and Youka Hayasaka.

This collection is dedicated to my father, Wilfredo Candano, who built bridges towards the acquisition of information that went into these stories.